BRIGHTWOOD SHADOWS

BRIGHTWOOD ACADEMY: SPY SCHOOL FOR TEENS

BRIGHTWOOD FILES
BOOK 1

KATHLEEN GUIRE

CHAPTER
ONE

DOWNTON ABBEY MEETS PSYCH

I WHEELED my clunky suitcase into the marble hall. I didn't belong here. This was a group home. A home for teens who had no parents. Or teens who'd broken the law.

I had a mother.

In prison for murder.

"Let me take your bags." An impeccably dressed butler reached for my suitcase.

He was tall and wiry, the kind of strong you don't expect from someone who looks like they iron their socks. His silver hair was slicked back like he belonged on the cover of some old British mystery novel. The black suit, white gloves, and polished shoes just made everything feel more surreal—like

I'd accidentally walked into a movie set instead of a group home.

"I'm Reginald Fairfax, butler of Brightwood Estate, you'll meet your hosts soon enough, Ellie Quinn." He grabbed the handle to my suitcase and rolled it across the cavernous hall. It clacked on the marble, the echo punctuating the size of Brightwood Estate.

"This is a group home?" I ventured as I passed a mirror, glancing in at my very out of place fiery red hair, freckles, and pale skin. I was fifteen years old and this was my first time away from home.

Homes — I'd lived all over the United States. Always the same neighborhood. A trailer park at the edge of town, adjacent to woods or whatever sort of wilderness that part of the country offered.

"Of sorts," Reginald offered with a chuckle. "Your hosts inherited this estate."

It seemed that is all he was going to say on the matter. We'd exhausted the hall and arrived at an elevator.

"All the guests' rooms are on the third floor." He clicked the button.

"All the guests?" I was confused. Where were the swarms of social workers and counselors? And the grungy accommodations? Broken-down wooden bunk beds shoved in one room? Tattered drunk house parents waiting for the check for fostering?

He pressed the third floor button. "Yes, there are three others at the moment."

The elevator hummed and the doors closed. It zipped up to the third floor in a matter of seconds. Once the door opened, Reginald shoved my suitcase off and said, "Dinner at six." He handed me a card that looked like a hotel key. "Room 304."

I stepped off the elevator in the direction he pointed and wheeled my suitcase to room 304. I waved the card over the door handle. The door buzzed and clicked. I turned the handle and paused. Surely I had a roommate. I wasn't sure I was ready for one.

It had always been just me and my mom. "Living off the grid," she called it. She homeschooled me. We spent all our time either learning, or training in the woods, or having fun. We'd lived in this mountain town a few hours outside of Washington D.C. for the last year. Until yesterday when officers showed up at our trailer and arrested her.

I wasn't one of these kids. I wasn't a foster kid. My mom didn't do drugs. She didn't drink. We had plenty of money, but in her words "you don't have to spend it all in one place."

I opened the door and blinked twice. My room had one queen sized bed and a bank of windows overlooking the backyard. A rug in evergreen, gold, and orange stretched across the dark floor, like even the carpet had to follow Brightwood's 'perfect aesthetic' rule. I wheeled my suitcase into the walk-in closet next to the dresser. The closet was empty. So I was the only occupant. Good. I needed time alone. I had one job: find out the truth about my mom—and try not to completely fall apart in this place while I was at it.

As I exited the closet, a voice in the hall asked, "Need anything, miss?"

A maid in a black and white uniform. Had I landed on the set of *Downton Abbey*? Wait. Was I supposed to dress for dinner?

I glanced around the room, and at the massive television mounted on the wall.

I tested the waters. "Uhhh, can I have a DVD player?"

"Of course, miss," she said. "I'll have one delivered to you."

"What should I wear to dinner?" I asked, and then looked down at my ripped jeans and oversized flannel over a tee shirt.

"I'm sure whatever you have on will be fine. I'll make sure you have a uniform delivered in the morning." With that, she stepped in the room, pulled a tape measure out of her pocket and whipped it around my waist, then shoulders. "Hold a leg out for me, dear."

I stuck a leg out and teetered as she measured my calf and thigh. What kind of group home was this?

"All done," she said. She shoved the tape measure

back in her apron pocket. "Reggie told you dinner at six, right? In the main hall."

"Reggie?"

"Reginald. We all call him Reggie."

"Yes. Where is the main hall?"

"Just take the elevator down to the main floor and walk to the back of the hall. Through the double doors. Can't miss it." She giggled. "I'm Maggie, by the way. If you need anything else, press this button." She motioned to a white button behind the door. "This red one is for emergencies only."

Emergencies? What sort of emergency could I have in this *Downton Abbey* group home?

"When do I meet the hosts?"

"The what, dear?" She paused and held her belly as she laughed. "Reggie's been playing up the butler role, has he? Vivian and Theo Lennox are your group home parents."

I breathed a sigh of relief. "I thought I'd stepped into an alternate universe."

She turned and walked briskly down the hallway, still laughing, "Reggie."

Once she was gone, I closed the door and examined my surroundings. There was a full bathroom with a shower and a fancy tub inside it. A pile of plush white towels sat on the sink vanity.

Back in the bedroom, I walked to the bank of windows. The yard below housed tennis courts, a pool, a gazebo, and a long lawn with a garden to rival Mr. Darcy's from Pride And Prejudice.

On the lawn were two teens, a girl with bright pink hair and a boy with blonde untamed hair, sticking out in all directions. The girl turned and saw me. She smiled and waved. The boy followed her gaze and did the same. I waved back and stepped away from the windows.

It was four o'clock. Two hours before dinner. Did I go down and meet them? There was a light knock at the door. I went to the door and tentatively opened it. A teen with dark skin and unruly curls and the most vibrant blue eyes I'd ever seen stared back at me. "Umm, Maggie said you wanted this." He held out a box with the words DVD Player on the side.

"Oh, yes, thank you. I want to watch my DVDs. I watched them with my…" I didn't finish the sentence because I wasn't sure what was group home appropriate.

"With your mom?" he finished for me. He moved into the room with a steady measured gate. "I'm Ezra. It's okay to talk about your mom. We all have stories."

He set the DVD Player down on the bed and lifted a pant leg. "Yeah, still getting used to these."

His leg was prosthetic.

"I have a matching one on the other leg." He smiled a sad smile. "Car accident."

Maybe that's how he lost his parents. I wasn't going to ask.

"Titanium?" I asked, admiring the technology.

"Yes, titanium legs are often lightweight and durable, allowing for a range of motion and functionality, but the gait will typically differ from a natural walk," he said as if he were reciting from a manual instead of describing his legs. "Let's get this set up."

He opened the box and the DVD Player squeaked as he freed it from the styrofoam. "So, you're old school?" He pulled out cords with yellow and red connectors.

"Yeah, my mom and I…" I paused again.

Her voice echoed in my head: *Don't trust easily, Ellie. Watch first. Listen always.*

The words buzzed like bees under my skin.

"I get it…" He paused. "What's your name?"

"Ellie," I replied. That's one thing I could reveal about myself. Not that it was my real name. My name changed every town we lived in. It was Ellie for now. I wasn't lying.

"We all have our quirks here. And if watching DVDs with your mom is part of your story, that's totally okay. Own it. What've you got?" He plugged the cords into the back of the TV.

"What?"

"Your DVDs. Show me what you have."

"Oh." I went to the closet, zipped open my suitcase and pulled out a set of *Psych* DVDs. I rejoined him at the TV. "This is what I have."

"Cool. Old school." He grabbed the set and opened the first season. "Mind if I…"

"Go right ahead."

He shoved the first one into the player and clicked play. I plopped down on a chair I'd pulled over to get a better view of the screen and he did the same.

For the next hour, I watched Psych with Ezra. He was the first teen boy I'd ever spent time with. I tried to be socially normal. Although I didn't know what that was. Of course, there was nothing socially normal about ending up in a group home because your mother committed murder or your parents died in a car crash leaving you to cope with titanium legs. Maybe it was time to just be myself.

Then my mother's voice played on the ticker tape of my mind again: *Blend in so well, they forget you were there.*

That's exactly what I planned to do. So I watched Ezra, learning his behaviors and mimicking his moves. Laughing when he laughed. Crossing my arms when he crossed his.

I couldn't get over those eyes though. As much as I tried not to stare at them, I was drawn to them. Like a bee to a flower. I wanted to get lost in them. Get a grip, Ellie. You're both misfits in a group home. This isn't some YA romcom. No happy ending here. Just serve your time, blend in, and find out what happened to your mom.

Then a thought hit me. "Hey Ezra, you're the tech guy around here, right?"

He smiled so big I thought his face was going to crack. His teeth were so white against his ebony skin. Stop it. Stop it. Focus. One tooth had a chip in it. Probably from the accident.

"Yes, I am. Thank you for noticing." He turned to face me, Shawn and Gus arguing on the screen in the background. "I don't usually hook up DVD Players."

"So you have a computer?"

"Don't you?"

"No. I don't even have a ph…" I stopped myself.

"Yeah, I have a computer lab downstairs in the basement."

"A lab? Like a lot of computers."

He chuckled. "If I didn't know any better, I'd say you time traveled here. Yes. A lot of computers."

"Could you help me do some research on the down low?"

"About?"

"My mom. I don't think she murdered anyone."

CHAPTER
TWO

PSYCH, TACOS, AND SECRET PASSAGES

AT DINNER, I was the only teen not wearing a uniform. Our group home parents, Vivian and Theo Lennox, were absent, which I thought odd. I ate every meal with my mom, and although I had no group home experience, I thought house parents were supposed to act like, well, parents.

The dining table in the main hall was so long, you needed walkie talkies like my mom and I used in training maneuvers in the woods to communicate from one end to the other. Not that anyone was sitting on the other end. Nope. We were all grouped at one end, with no one daring to sit at the head of the table. Sitting at the head of the table was a power move, one none of these teens were willing to make.

Reginald, or Reggie as everyone called him,

buzzed around the table instructing the staff as they served before vanishing into the woodwork. Literally. Through a large wooden door invisible to the naked eye until he pushed a button under the buffet and it swung open. I watched in wide-eyed wonder and then quickly fixed my expression to match Ezra's. One side of me wanted to explore and see what else this house had hidden. Or secret places I could hide away. The other part of me wanted to solely focus on the goal and get my mom out of prison so we could go home and hide away together.

Once the staff had left, we four teens ate in silence for what seemed an eternity. Which suited me just fine. Although I missed my mother and wanted her back desperately, she had a habit, like Shawn's dad Henry from *Psych*, of quizzing me while we were eating.There were no quiet dinners in my trailer. Mom rattled off scenarios and I answered with how I would blend in or escape.

"So… I'm Annabelle Phoenix" Annabelle began, breaking the silence. "New girl, what's your name?"

"Ellie Quinn." I couldn't stop staring at her fuchsia hair. She had the most perfect Asian skin I'd ever seen.

She flipped a section of it with her butter knife. "Like it? I say show them what you've got. You know. Stand out."

The blond boy I'd seen out the window laughed, eyeing my bright red hair. "I think Ellie's got you beat in the stand-out hair department." He stood and bowed. "Cory Wilder at your service."

"And you've met me," Ezra added as he shoved some ground beef back onto his taco.

"What's your story?" Annabelle prodded.

Ezra shoved a tortilla chip in his mouth and chewed three times before saying, "Go easy on her. This is all new to her."

I picked up my napkin and wiped my lips. "I don't belong here. I'm not staying."

I looked around the dining hall in case an adult came out of the woodwork and heard what I was saying.

I leaned forward and whispered, "My mom was accused of murder. She didn't do it and I'm going to prove it, get out of here and go home." I stood and threw my napkin on my plate. I wasn't some group home kid and telling these teens my life story so they could twist it and use it against me wasn't going to happen. I'd already told Ezra too much. I was going to my room to watch more *Psych* and then take a bath.

"Where are you going?" Ezra asked.

"Back to my room. Do we have to stay here?"

"Nope. We don't have anything until tomorrow morning," he answered. "But I thought you might want to start clearing your mother's name."

I paused. "You mean you'll get on your computer and help me research?"

Cory stifled a laugh. "You mean wall of computers."

Annabelle stood and whispered to Cory, "Keep quiet. I don't think she's had her briefing or entrance exams."

I didn't just hear them—I watched every glance, every shift, every flicker they didn't think I'd notice. Sure, I might not know how to act normal around a hot teen guy, but reading people? That I could do. My mom made sure of it. And right now? This group was definitely hiding something. I didn't know if this was the Lord Of The Flies Group Home mentality and I was about to go through some sort of hazing tonight or not. I opted for not.

"Nope. I think I'll turn in early." I walked across the dining hall before turning and asking, "What's tomorrow morning?"

"Life skills," Ezra said quietly. "We meet for breakfast, then go shopping or...whatever they have planned. Just to show we can handle normal stuff."

"No school?" I asked, trying not to sound as clueless as I felt. I'd been homeschooled my whole life, but I was pretty sure most kids went to public or private school—at least in the normal world.

"This is part of school," Cory said. "Vivian and Theo have tutors and counselors on staff. We learn everything we need to here. Or out in the fie—"

Annabelle jabbed her fist into his stomach and

instead of finishing his sentence, a whoosh of air escaped, followed by, "What the heck, Annabelle?"

"She hasn't met Vivian or Theo yet," she said through gritted teeth. "And you heard her. She doesn't belong here. Probably won't be here long enough …" Again the words trailed off.

There was something fishy about this place, and not a "group home, poor foster kids" fishy. I didn't want to stay here long enough to find out what kind of fishy. I ran to the elevator and pushed the button.

All I wanted was to disappear into my room. But then I saw my mom in my head—alone in that cell. I could almost feel the cold concrete pressing up through her thin mattress, smell that sour, damp stink mixed with something sharp and bitter, like skunk spray that clings no matter how hard you try to wash it out. The light buzzed and flickered overhead, one wire holding it like it might snap any second. No TV. No books. No sound except her own breathing—and no me.

I turned on my heel and headed back to the dining room. I'd tell Ezra I'd changed my mind. But when I got there, not only was the dining room empty, but the staff hadn't cleaned up yet. I assumed that's what they did – I may be a fan of *Psych*, but I'd rented the whole set of *Downton Abbey* DVDS from the library once. I did what any self-respecting teen would do: I ignored the mess and went straight for the button to open the door in the wall. I pressed it and I slipped through to a dimly lit hallway.

The hallway led to a wide set of stairs. I tiptoed down them, barely breathing, like the floor might rat me out. At the bottom, I landed in what felt like an Alice in Wonderland moment—minus the shrinking potion and creepy tea party. Just a bunch of closed doors. All of them looked the same. No signs, no hints, no clues. Just choices. And every choice led to a locked door. I tried them all, one by one, my hand sweating on each cold knob. Where was everybody? They hadn't gone upstairs—I would've seen them pass me. It was like they'd vanished.

Were there more hidden doors and passages in the mansion? I heard voices coming toward me and the distinct clacking of heels on the marble floor. I slipped under the stairway and hid.

"Have you briefed Caroline Quinn's daughter?" a male voice asked.

"No, Theo. I haven't had time," a woman's voice answered, which I assumed was Vivian.

"You mean, you don't want to."

"Of course I don't want to. Cheyenne is dead. We killed a teen, Theo, and look at Ezra. He…"

A beeping sound followed by the sound of a door opening and closing ended the conversation.

As soon as I was sure they were well inside, I beelined it up the stairs, back to the hallway. As I opened the door in the wall, I smacked into Reggie.

"Everything all right, my dear?" He peered behind me as if I was being chased.

"Yeah, sure. Just not feeling great." I put both hands on my knees and sucked in a deep breath. "So the life skills tomorrow. Is it, umm…mandatory?"

"Not if you aren't feeling well. We can give you a day off to settle in." He smiled and patted me on the shoulder.

I stood up and took a deep breath to compose myself. "But if I change my mind?"

"We will take the bus at the corner at 8 am and each teen is to go shopping in town for groceries."

That's it? No secret covert mission? No assassinations?

"Cool, thanks."

"Would you like breakfast delivered to your room?"

"I can do that?"

"Just this one time, and it will be our little secret. Take the morning off."

"Thanks," I said.

I was not taking the morning off. Step one: find out what was going on. Step two: get my mom out of prison. Step three: make it out alive.

As I walked across the dining hall, Reggie called after me, "Oh, my dear, there's a group counseling session after lunch. That's mandatory."

"Yes, sir." I zipped across the marble floor, got on

the waiting elevator and went to my room and locked the door.

That overheard conversation? It had flipped a switch. A part of me I'd tucked away, labeled *things I'll never need,* was now buzzing like a live wire.

I scanned the room for cameras. Found none. Then I unzipped the hidden flap in my suitcase and pulled out a bug detector—one of the tools Joan had made me practice with, back when I thought she was just paranoid. Or maybe prepping me for a future I'd never live.

I found three bugs and left them. If I started dismantling my room, they'd be on to me faster than a fly on honey.

I'd brushed off most of Mom and Joan's "someday you'll need this" speeches as paranoia, but that conversation had the same sharp, electric thrum as the day Joan made me spot a tail through a crowded farmer's market. Brightwood's perfect room suddenly felt wrong—like it was *watching me back.*

I turned on the TV and pressed play on the DVD player and let *Psych* run in the background while I made a plan for the morning. If I knew anything about teens — what was I saying? I knew nothing about teens. Only what I'd learned through DVDS and what my mom had told me, which wasn't much. It was more along the lines of: don't trust anyone. Don't tell anyone your real name. "Blend in so well, they forget you were there" was her mantra. And that's exactly what I was going to do when I went on the little life skills trip tomorrow morning.

CHAPTER
THREE

PSYCH MEETS ALIAS, SENIOR CITIZEN EDITION

"IT'S TOO bad Ellie couldn't come," Ezra lamented as he, Annabelle, Cory, and a crimped and bent old lady waited for the bus.

That would be me. I was the little old lady. I stood away from the group and after waiting for five minutes, sat down on the bench. That's what an eighty-five year old would do, right? Sit on the bench and wait for the bus, all the while listening in to the conversation. I'd added the little details to my disguise, such as a bit of cat hair on my sweater and a generous spritz of perfume.

"It's better this way," Annabelle said, as she twirled her hair around her fingers. She smacked her bright pink lips. "She hasn't been briefed yet. And you heard her. She doesn't belong here."

Cory chuckled and adjusted his hoodie zipper. "What's the mission today? I know it's not that life skills crap you were spewing at her last night."

He threw a quick glance at me. "Sorry, ma'am."

I smiled, cracking my make-up, adding a few more wrinkles. I'm sure he was apologizing for the word "crap" which he most likely used instead of another expletive on my account.

Old people are invisible. No one sees them. Or pays attention to them until they do something they think their grandma would disapprove of. Despite the apology, the teens kept talking as if I weren't there.

"Who has the mish information?"Cory continued.

Annabelle flicked imaginary dirt off her perfectly polished nail. "The mish has changed since Katniss Everdeen isn't coming."

Ezra leaned on the lamppost, his discomfort evident."How do you know that? Did you get the mission directive?"

Cory turned to face Ezra, concern evident on his face. "Listen dude, you maybe should go back to Brightwood. You don't look so good."

I studied his profile. Beads of sweat formed on his forehead. "I'm fine, still getting used to these." He knocked on his calf.

"Well, you don't usually do field work," Annabelle explained. "You stay in the computer lab or van and in our ears."

"Why am I here?"

"Theo wants you to come."

At that point, Ezra sat down next to me on the bench. I gave him a quick smile and pulled a tissue from my purse, blowing my nose loud enough to turn heads. Another one of my mom's tricks—if people got too close, give them a reason to back off.

Ezra shifted, his hands fidgeting with the hem of his jacket. "Theo's been… stepping in more lately," he said quietly. "Since Reggie—" He hesitated. "Since Cheyenne didn't make it back and I… well, you know. Reggie hasn't exactly been himself. Theo says he's helping, but it feels different now. Like he's running things."

"What is taking the bus so long?" Annabelle bounced on her tiptoes and looked up and down the street. With no bus in sight, she turned to Ezra. "You sure you're up for this, or you going to stay with the old lady and talk about surgeries and ailments?"

Ezra stood, steadying himself with one hand on the bus bench. "That was uncalled for. Apologize to her and tell me what the mission is."

"I'm sorry cat lady," Annabelle said quickly before turning back to the approaching bus.

As the bus door hissed open, Annabelle added, "This is a simple info gathering mission."

Mission. Field work. Information gathering. What had I landed myself in the middle of? These weren't regular foster kids—they were being trained for something. But clearly, nobody had covered the part where you don't spill mission details in front of random old ladies.

Annabelle blended in as well as a sequined Vegas singer in a convent. Cory could pass as a regular teen, a jock with his blonde hair and defined muscles, including his football player broad shoulders. Ezra seemed to be the brains of the operation. And whatever had happened to his legs hadn't happened years ago but a lot more recently.

Although I wanted to know more about him and the teen, Cheyenne, Vivian and Theo confessed to killing, I wasn't going to abort the mission: find out who set my mom up to take the blame for murder, get her exonerated, and leave Brightwood in the rearview mirror.

I hobbled up the stairs and slid in a seat behind Ezra.

The bus groaned to life and pulled back into traffic.

"What would we be doing if Ellie had come along?" Cory asked.

Annabelle pulled a mirror out and reapplied her lipstick. "A life skills shopping trip."

Cory folded his arms across his chest. "For real?"

"We aren't supposed to talk about what we do until she's been briefed, trained, and tested," Ezra explained.

"She's some sort of off-the-grid Katniss type.

Homeschooled her whole life." Annabelle paused, like she wanted the words to sound dramatic but couldn't quite pull it off. "I mean, look at her. She's right—she doesn't belong with us. We're... we're supposed to be the best of the best."

"So was Cheyenne," Ezra whispered, wiping a tear from his eye. "Maybe you're just afraid Ellie's going to outshine you."

"Don't be so emo, Ezra. Cheyenne—" Annabelle's voice faltered for half a second before she scanned the bus, then dropped her voice lower. "Cheyenne messed up. She didn't follow protocol. And now...she's not here anymore."

"You guys are talking too much," Cory cut in. "Wake me up when we get there." He leaned back, pulled his hood up, and shut down.

Ezra and Annabelle didn't say anything either. They just stared out the window, looking bored and a little checked out. After three stops, I realized the bus route seemed familiar. Two more stops in this direction would lead us to the edge of town and my trailer park.

Two stops later, Annabelle signaled for Ezra and shook Cory who had been sitting next to her. "This is our stop."

I clutched my purse and followed them as they exited the bus.

This was awkward. We were the only people exiting. The trailer park wasn't that large and backed up against a nature reserve. I couldn't exactly show up at a neighbor's house in this get-up. Who was I kidding? I couldn't show up at a neighbor's house because I didn't know any neighbors. Except one. Joan. Mom's long-time friend. My godmother.

I stumbled along on the gravel, pretending I was confused. Looking at each trailer number.

Cory led the group, his hands shoved in the front pockets of his hoodie. He scanned the trailer park, his head shifting back and forth. I was behind them so I couldn't see his expression. But that's when I got it. He's the muscle.

"And when are you going to tell us what the mission *is*. Exactly."

Ezra turned to face me. "Are you lost, ma'am?"

I shook my head in the negative and tottered off between two trailers. Darn. I wasn't going to hear what the real mission was. Then it hit me. This was my trailer park – Shadow Pines. If the police were finished with my home, which I'm sure they were, I could go home. Maybe I could stay here. Live by myself until I brought my mom home. I knew how to live off the grid, fly under the radar. No one would ever know I was here.

I could sneak back to the group home later and grab all my stuff. This was going to work. Excited by my plan, I forgot for a moment that I was dressed like Miss Marple and took off at a jog. As I rounded the corner to my block, I skidded to a stop like a cartoon character and froze.

Ezra, Annabelle, and Cory were standing on Joan's porch — the trailer right next to mine. She was yelling at them in a controlled whispery what-the-heck way.

"What are you doing here? You shouldn't be here." She grabbed Annabelle by the arm and pulled her toward the door. "Get inside. All of you. Were you followed?"

"Of course not," Cory said as she pushed him inside.

Joan stood on the porch half a second longer, her gaze sweeping the trailer park like she was cataloging every piece of it. Then her eyes locked on mine. I froze, like a deer caught in headlights. She recognized me—I felt it in the pit of my stomach. For a split second, something cold flickered behind her smile—like she was sizing me up—but it was gone before I could pin it down. The bright, familiar godmother smile returned, soft and polished. She lifted her hand and motioned for me to come, her eyes never letting go of mine.

Since the jig was up, I jogged to the porch and slipped in the front door.

"Is this your grandma?" Cory asked. "She was kind of lost out there."

Clearly, Cory wasn't the brains.

"You weren't followed, huh?" Joan said as she

whipped my wig off my head, exposing a hair net which she grabbed as well. My bright red hair tumbled out onto my shoulders.

Annabelle's eyes were as wide as a grande Starbuck's coffee lid.

Cory chuckled and Ezra smiled.

"I knew she was one of us," Ezra said in a way of congratulations. He gave a quick sideways glance to Annabelle and gave her a satisfying smug smile. Satisfying for me anyway. I could look at that smile all day. And I was so glad to be besting Annabelle, or Katnissing her, or whatever the kids called it these days.

Then it dawned on me. I'd been judging Cory for being the dumb one. All the while, it had been me. Joan — she'd moved every time we had. She always lived next door. These kids weren't just foster kids. They were spies.

"You're my mom's handler."

Joan nodded and added, "I'm your handler too."

ALIAS MEETS THE HUNGER GAMES, WITH A SIDE OF TOTALLY SPIES

"I'M NOT A SPY."

Joan ignored my statement and glared at Annabelle, Cory, and Ezra. "Who assigned you this mission?"

Ezra leaned up against a ratty green upholstered chair, clearly uncomfortable. Was it from messing up, or the new prosthetics? Or the fact that I was a spy? I couldn't tell.

"Theo. There was a card in Annabelle's box this morning. She logged in to the number given and ended up here."

Joan wasn't finished, her dark cheeks pinked. "What was the mission?"

Annabelle was clearly annoyed, evidenced by the

disdain circling her puckered pink lips. She jutted a hip out to the side. "Gather intel. simple."

Joan shot back, "You came to a trailer park dressed like that?" She waved a hand up and down at Annabelle's tight mini skirt and hot pink sweater, stopping at her hair.

"Well, Ellie here is dressed as Miss Marple." She shot me a look of disgust.

"And she fits right in," Cory pointed out, followed by a chuckle.

I smiled despite the weight of the situation. Maybe it was an avoidance smile.Whatever. Without realizing it, Cory had taken my side. He wasn't trying to make things better—just trying to make them *stop*. Classic avoidance move. I knew it because I'd done it, too.

The whole thing felt unreal. But the pieces were stacking up.

My mom was a spy and Joan was her handler. These teens were spies. And I was sent to Brightwood for training. What kind of spies? I'd never seen my mom leave in the middle of the night. She didn't leave the country. We barely left the neighborhood. A fuzzy memory surfaced. One of Joan watching Totally Spies with me and my mom leaving. She was gone for days.

"Did my mom murder Senator Malcolm Rusk?"

"Let me get some refreshments and we'll have a conversation." Joan walked around the trailer and pulled all the blinds closed before stepping into the kitchen.

My mission hadn't changed. I didn't want to be a spy. And as far as my memories told me, she'd quit the business years ago, when we started moving around. After my father left us, we sold the house and moved into a trailer park. It was such a common story of divorce, I hadn't questioned it. I was five at the time. Now the scenes played across my mental screen again and they looked a lot different. More like a thriller full of spies, deceit, and life on the run. I didn't want any part of it.

Joan pulled energy drinks out of the fridge, and held two up. "These okay? My one weakness."

Before she enunciated the "s," I heard a crackling sound followed by a buzzing past my ear. Joan gasped and crumpled to the ground.

"Hit the floor," I commanded.

We hit the floor and I landed next to Ezra, who was shaking. Annabelle's look of disgust had been replaced by fear...or was that anger? Cory pushed himself up to a plank position. So my earlier inclination had been right. He was the muscle. The protection. The enforcer, or whatever.

I crawled over to Joan. There were no last-minute instructions. No speech on how much my mother loved me and what to do next. No. The bullet hit the mark on her forehead. She was gone. The energy drinks rolled on the linoleum floor beside her.

The precise hit was the work of a professional assassin.

"Do you have a weapon?" I hissed to Cory.

"No, this was a simple recon." His playful demeanor shifted into spy mode.

"I know where we can get some." I shut Joan's eyes. Although I wanted to burst into tears and cry over my godmother, like Cory, my training kicked in. I didn't dare look out the windows. Obviously the bullet was sent to silence Joan. But maybe I was also a target, and this group of teen misfit spies as well.

I rolled over to the ratty green chair and shoved it aside just as another bullet tore through the upholstery. My wool tights snagged on the shag carpet as I found the handle and yanked. These tights were officially dead—first chance we got, they were going in the trash.

I glanced back. Ezra had crawled toward the kitchen island, closer to Joan and Annabelle, crouched near the back wall. Good. He was out of the line of fire.

Another bullet hit an energy drink can, which exploded like a tiny soda bomb, spinning in wild circles and misting the cabinets with green apple fizz. The tangy sugar mixed with the sharp, metallic scent of blood, and my stomach lurched.

"I told her those weren't good for her," I whispered, trying to lighten the mood as I motioned for Ezra to join me and slip down the rabbit hole. That's what Joan had called it. It was a game we had played: she'd say the word "rabbit" and time me as I climbed down the hole. I'd been so stupid. Mom and Joan had been training me all along. All the games. The detective shows like *Psych*. Mom's mantra: *Blend in so well, they forget you were there.*

Ezra struggled with the ladder and landed on the rabbit hole floor on his bottom with a thump. "I'm okay," he reported.

"Cory, go down and help him. Go left," I instructed.

Cory army crawled to the hole and scrambled down the ladder.

"Got him," he whispered to me.

"Come on, Ezra. Let's go," he continued to Ezra as they shuffled down the hallway.

"If you think I'm going to let you tell me what to do…I'm a trained spy. You're a…" Annabelle waved her hand at me, which from her position on her stomach was awkward.

"Listen," I answered through gritted teeth. "I'm not going to have your death on my hands."

As if to punctuate my statement, another bullet whizzed through the broken window and shattered a cheap cabinet front.

Annabelle slithered over and climbed down the ladder. Before she disappeared, she gave me one last look of contempt. Her perfectly groomed eyebrows squished together like two angry caterpillars. I followed, then led them down the tight corridor that opened into a hobbit-like room.

"This is your secret lair?" Annabelle asked, scanning the dirt floor.

"No, this is my weapons cache," I said.

Annabelle opened her mouth to speak, but Cory cut her off, nodding toward the weapons wall. "Crossbow, Katniss. Nice."

"Where are the guns?" Annabelle interjected.

I flipped my shoes off, jerked the tights down and flung them into a corner. As I pulled a pair of leggings out of a cupboard, I answered, "No guns."

I yanked the leggings up over my legs, the fabric stretching tight but smooth, like armor I didn't have to buckle. They were black, the kind of black that didn't reflect light, the kind that meant business. Reinforced knees, stitched like someone expected me to crawl through gravel. Probably because I had.

The waistband hugged my hips just right—snug, secure. No slouchy fabric to snag on branches or get in my way. I slipped my fingers into the side pocket, just to check my extra string and the hex key were still there. They were. Good.

I tugged the hem down over my boots and did a few squats, half out of habit, half out of nerves. These leggings moved with me, silent and steady. Like they knew I needed to disappear into the trees and hit a target dead center. No excuses. No noise. Just me, the crossbow, and whatever waited on the other side of the woods. Except this time, I had three other people to think about.

Once I had the pants on, I pulled the dress off, followed by the mask.

"What do you want me to do?" Ezra asked.

"Stay here." I tossed the slip I wore under the dress on the floor and swapped into a T-shirt and a camo hunting shirt—long-sleeved, button-down, layered like a hunter ready to move.

"What are you going to do?" Cory asked.

"Do you know how to shoot one of these?" I grabbed a crossbow.

"I think so."

Not ideal—but still better than Annabelle. She hadn't even touched the crossbow, and with that neon-pink hair, she stuck out like a flamingo in a herd of deer. First rule of hunting: blend in. She'd be picked off faster than an eight-point buck in a clearing.

"What's the plan?" Cory continued as he fiddled with the bow.

"You're going to get the assassin out in the clearing," I said as I slung a quiver over my camo shirt.

"And you?" he asked.

"I'm going to wound the assassin. So we can question him or her."

"I'm not staying here." Annabelle looked around the room, her gaze landing on a camo jump suit. "I'll put this on."

We didn't have time for this. If I waited for her to get dressed, the assassin could be gone. But Annabelle didn't miss a beat. She was dressed in the jumpsuit and a green beanie before I could say no.

I motioned for Cory to join me and I opened the door to the woods.

———

The woods pressed in around me, silent and heavy, as if holding its breath. I crouched behind the wide trunk of an oak tree, the crossbow cold and solid in my hands. My heart thudded hard, echoing in my ears, and I tried to steady my breathing. Annabelle knelt beside me, her face unreadable—until she reached up and tugged off her hat.

"Annabelle, what are you doing?" I hissed, my voice barely above a whisper.

She turned to me with a sly smile and shook out her bright pink hair. "What I do best—being bait."

Before I could stop her, she darted out into the clearing, her hair like a neon target against the muted greens and browns of the woods. My stomach flipped. What if the assassin shot her through the forehead, like he'd just done with Joan? What if—

"Relax." Cory's voice was calm and measured. He crept through the woods to an ancient oak tree. He mouthed, "I'm in position. Moving up."

I paused long enough to watch him climb a tree

about twenty feet away. His movements were smooth and precise, his black hoodie blending into the shadows as he disappeared into the branches.

"Eyes on him," Cory said loudly. "Northwest, thirty meters. He's moving."

I shifted, keeping low, and peered through the crossbow's sight. The assassin was a dark shape moving between the trees, his focus locked on Annabelle as she stumbled, letting out a convincing yelp. My chest tightened, and I gripped the crossbow harder.

"Hold steady, Ellie," I told myself. "You've got this."

The assassin moved closer, drawn by Annabelle's act. She zigzagged through the clearing, her pink hair bobbing as she pretended to trip over a root. He didn't see Cory up in the trees, and he definitely didn't know I had him in my crossbow scope.

"Now or never," I told myself. I'd only used this crossbow on a deer. Not a man.

I sucked in a breath and steadied my aim. My palms were slick, but I focused on the bolt, lining it up with the assassin's shoulder. Not lethal. Just enough to take him out of the game.

The crossbow string snapped, and the bolt flew.

He spun as it hit, letting out a sharp cry before collapsing against a tree, clutching his shoulder. Relief surged through me, but it was fleeting. Cory's voice cut in, sharp and urgent.

"Move!"

Annabelle bolted back toward me, her pink hair a blur. Cory dropped from the tree with a heavy thud, landing on his feet like he'd done it a hundred times before. I stayed frozen for a second, my eyes locked on the assassin as he slumped against the trunk, groaning.

I exhaled shakily and lowered the crossbow, my hands trembling.

"Stay down," I muttered, half to him, half to myself.

Annabelle skidded to a stop beside me, her breathing ragged but her grin infuriatingly wide. "Told you I'd make a good distraction."

Cory joined us, brushing dirt from his jeans and glaring across the woods at the assassin.

"Nice shot, Ellie," he said. "But next time, maybe let me climb higher before you take it."

I couldn't help it—I laughed. It was short and nervous, but it was real. For now, we had the upper hand. But deep down, I knew this wasn't over. Not yet.

CHAPTER
FIVE

PSYCH MEETS THE BOURNE IDENTITY, TRAILER PARK EDITION

I SLUNG the bow over my shoulder and jogged over to the tree where the assassin had slumped after my arrow had found its mark in his shoulder.

There was no one there. A crimson stain soaked into the bark of the tree. I reached in my pocket and pulled out a tissue. I gently picked up the broken arrow. By then, Cory and Annabelle had joined me.

I held out the arrow. "Can Ezra lift the fingerprints off this?"

Instead of answering, Cory scanned the field. "Want me to track him?"

"No." I didn't want to have Cory's death on my hands. Then I'd never get out of the group home.

Annabelle gazed at where the man had fallen and

quickly adjusted her expression to a bored static look. It was evident that she and the rest of the group had recently survived a horrific tragedy which ended in Ezra losing his legs from below the knee and Cheyenne losing her life.

"Of course he can," Annabelle said. She turned on her heel. "This isn't the 1800s Hunger Games, girl. Nice shot by the way."

"Hunger Games took place in the future," Cory corrected her, and then added, "That guy couldn't have gotten far. Sure you don't want me to go after him?"

"She said no," Annabelle said, a little too quickly.

Sirens screamed into the trailer park.

"What are we going to do?" Cory asked.

"We can't go back to the trailer park. Not right now. And not dressed like this." I nodded toward Annabelle's camo jump suit.

"Yes, I wouldn't be caught dead like this," Annabelle said, then covered her mouth and swallowed.

"Ezra!" I turned and ran toward our bunker/hobbit hole.

Cory and Annabelle followed.

I arrived at the door, out of breath, and took a minute to compose myself before slipping inside with Cory and Annabelle following. Once the door was secured, I checked on Ezra.

"I made sure the door to Joan's was secure and the carpet moved back while you were gone."

"Good job, Ezra. We'll have to be quiet for a while and then you three are going to tell me all about Brightwood Estate and what is going on that involves my mom."

I sat down on a crate and waited in silence while the police did their thing . I studied Annabelle, Cory, and Ezra.

"Stop staring," Annabelle whispered. "That's creepy. I feel like you are reading my thoughts."

I made my eyes as wide as possible. "Maybe I am."

I turned to see Ezra grinning. Cory had leaned against a cabinet and was snoozing. I'd have to give him a kick if he started snoring. The last thing we wanted was the police hauling in a bunch of foster kids who'd just been in Joan's trailer. Her death hadn't hit me yet. I knew it would. Blocking out everything else was something I excelled at. I'm sure part of it could be attributed to my training with my mom. And part of it was my nature or survival mode. Whatever you called it, I could focus on the moment, block out my emotions, until days later when they came bubbling up like hot molten lava threatening to blow.

Right now, the ability to block my feelings was a gift I planned to use to my advantage. My mom and Joan had been targeted. Mom blamed for a crime she didn't commit. Joan murdered. And somehow it was tied to Brightwood…or was it?

In the show, *Psych*, this is the point that Shawn found some way to weasel his way into a case. This is the point that mom, if she weren't in jail, would pack us up and move us to another trailer park in a new town. We'd change our names and start over. The story was always different: Recently divorced. Running from an abusive husband. Widowed.

This was my story. I was the main character in a show I didn't sign up for.

"I think they've gone," Cory said, interrupting my thoughts. "Want me to go check?"

I stood and wiped the dust off my leggings. "Can you do it without being noticed?"

"Send me and I'll get some information to boot," Annabelle offered.

"Cory, go, and don't let anyone see you."

Cory was out of the door before Annabelle could object.

"You really don't know how trailer parks work, do you, Annabelle?"

She moved way too close in my personal space and jabbed a finger in my chest. "Everyone knows everyone and everyone talks."

"Yes," I said, backing up, my butt landing on a crate.

It shattered, making a loud cracking noise. I froze, waiting for someone to rush in and arrest us.

Ezra maneuvered his way between us.

"I think what Ellie is saying is you need to recognize her strengths and use them like we did yours."

Annabelle stood her ground, puffing out her chest. "She is not in charge of me. She's not even a trained spy."

Then it hit me: Cheyenne was in charge of the team. The girl who died. And here I was showing up and getting into the middle of things.

I stood and dusted myself off. "Fine. Don't listen. I don't want to be in charge."

The door opened and Cory slipped back in. "We can leave. We will have to be careful though." He laughed and then added, "The police are going door to door asking about an old woman who was seen entering Joan's trailer."

"Ha! See! See!" Annabelle declared triumphantly. "You tried to blend in and you stood out like a sore thumb."

"That's not all," Cory interrupted. "And three teens. So we'll leave as four teens. Does that work?"

"No, it doesn't. I'm not leaving. You three go back to Brightwood Estate and do your spying or whatever you do there. I'm staying here. In my trailer."

Ezra patted me on the back. "We get it. You want to find out what happened and get your mom out of jail. But I think the answers to your questions are at Brightwood."

"Let her stay here and live in the woods and eat

those things that fall off Maple Trees. Acorns. And shoot deer with her bow," Annabelle huffed.

"Oak trees," I corrected.

Ezra put a hand on Annabelle's shoulder. He stood between us with a hand on each of us. "Annabelle, Ellie is not trying to replace Cheyenne."

A tear dripped down Annabelle's face and she wiped it away with the camo jumper sleeve.

Cory wiggled the door handle to get our attention. "Guys, we need to go. The bus stops at the entrance in seven minutes."

"If you stay here, you won't know why your mom wanted you at Brightwood," Ezra said as the three exited.

I stood alone for thirty seconds. What if Ezra was right? My mom wanted me at Brightwood Estates for a reason. She was a spy. Maybe she'd been training me for the same position all these years.

I slipped out the door and ran, taking a shortcut through the woods. I arrived at the bus stop, out of breath just as the bus pulled up. Ezra caught my eye and smiled. Annabelle turned and followed his gaze. When she saw me, she puckered up her face like an upset toddler and stomped up the steps onto the bus. Cory waited for me to get on the bus, then gave me a hearty slap on the back, sending me spiraling forward. I grabbed the handrail. "Glad you're joining us, Ellie."

Ezra followed and plopped down in the seat next

to me. "Mind if I sit down, Miss Marple? Can't believe you fooled us all."

Cory leaned forward from the seat behind us. "Wait until Reggie hears this!"

I gave him a look. "Reggie already knows. Or at least, he should."

"The butler," Annabelle added with a giggle, like it was still some inside joke.

Ezra smirked. "The butler routine's for the newbies. You know Reggie's more than that."

I did. Reggie ran Brightwood. Which was exactly why none of this made sense.

He wasn't the type to sign off on a mission like this. Not one where we walked blind into an ambush that could've gotten all of us killed. So why did he let Theo call the shots?

Theo was technically new, but somehow he'd pulled the strings on this op. And for what? What were we even supposed to gather at Joan's trailer? Theo had said "intel," but there hadn't been any. Not unless you counted walking straight into an assassin's line of fire as useful data.

Unless that was the point.

My stomach twisted. Was the whole thing a setup? A test? Or something worse?

WHEN THERAPY GOES FULL MISSION IMPOSSIBLE

ONCE BACK AT BRIGHTWOOD, I looked at the mansion with a new perspective. It loomed ahead as we walked through the gates, the familiar ivy-covered stone looking a little less welcoming than before.

I glanced at Ezra. "Are Theo and Vivian spies too?"

He pushed the gate open, letting it clang shut behind us. "Vivian was. Theo's new. He married her six months ago and moved onto the estate."

"So he didn't know she was running a training center for spies until after they got married?" I asked, my voice tight.

Ezra exhaled slowly, like he was weighing how much to say. "That's what he claims. But ever since

Reggie's been… struggling, Theo's kind of stepped up. Or taken over. Depends how you look at it."

The sidewalk stretched ahead like it was getting longer with every step. The weight of Joan's death—and everything she'd handed me—dragged at my legs. I wanted nothing more than to curl up in my room, pop in a *Psych* DVD, and pretend none of this existed. Pretend I hadn't just promised to come back.

"I don't know. Good question, man," Cory said. "That's why we need you, on account of you and Ezra have the brains."

Annabelle huffed.

"But you have the beauty," he added quickly.

She smiled. "That's right. When you can stand out like I do…"

Her smile slipped and was replaced by…what was that? Fear?

Something like a warning flag popped up in my brain as we entered the double doors.

"Ahhh, Miss Ellie, I see you decided to join in on the mission," Reggie said in greeting. Then he looked at our hands. "Where are the items you were to procure?"

"This was supposed to be another shopping trip?" Annabelle stomped her foot. "We are spies, Reggie."

Reggie glanced at me, watching my expression carefully.

"She knows everything," Ezra said.

"Yeah and her mom's handler is dead," Cory added.

Reggie straightened his back and looked from face to face."What?"

"Can you debrief us later?" Annabelle asked with a hand on her hip. "I'm beat."

That red flag that had popped up a few seconds ago was now waving like it was in hurricane force winds. As we waited for a reply, I thought back over what I'd learned so far about this place: Ezra had been seriously injured in an accident. Cheyenne was dead. Reggie had been sending the teens on shopping trips instead of missions. It didn't seem as if anyone had trained as extensively as I had, but I may be jumping to conclusions there. That was yet to be seen.

"Lunch in half an hour," Reggie said, and turned on his heel and marched away, his butler persona back in place.

Half an hour wasn't long enough for a *Psych* episode, but long enough for a shower. Instead of waiting for the elevator, I ran up the three flights of stairs, eager to get to my room. I was probably being rude. I didn't care. Right now, I wanted to be alone. I didn't ask to be on this team. All I knew was I had three priorities: figure out how to help my mom, untangle whatever secrets Brightwood was sitting on, and—maybe—spend more time with Ezra.

That last one? Optional. Probably dangerous. But still.

As I rounded the corner to my room and pulled the key out of my pocket, I bumped into Ezra and sent him reeling backwards. That was not a romcom move. I grabbed his hand just in time and pulled him back up.

He steadied himself by leaning on the wall. There was no witty banter like between Shawn and Julia on *Psych*. As I swiped the room key, it buzzed and clicked. I opened the door.

"Mind if I come in?" he asked.

"I'm really tired and emotionally spent." I paused. "But yeah, for a minute."

I plopped down on a chair and he did the same. The door behind us was still open. I stood to shut it—Ezra hadn't said a word, but I'd caught the wince when he sat, the way his hands hovered on the armrests like he was bracing. If he noticed the open door, he'd probably get up to close it himself. Just to prove he could. I beat him to it.

"Is Ezra already here?" Annabelle entered before I could close the door.

"I'm here," Cory said as he ran in and plopped on the bed. "Let's get this party started."

I guess we were having a meeting...or party. I didn't know which.

"So you've been training to be a spy your whole life," Cory began.

I plopped on the floor and sat cross-legged. "No. I have been living off the grid my whole life learning how to survive."

"That's so cool, man," Cory said.

"No offense, Ellie, but most people don't need to be able to shoot a crossbow like Katniss Everdeen to survive," Ezra added.

"You do if you want to live off the grid and survive."

Annabelle tapped her pinked cheek with her forefinger. "So you lived in a trailer park and Joan was your handler."

"I lived in a trailer park, but I didn't know until today that Joan was my handler. Guys, she is my godmother. I didn't know I was training to be a spy."

Cory laughed so hard he rolled off the bed. "And you guys call me the dumb one."

I sucked in a deep breath and tried to not throw everyone out of the room.

"Listen," Annabelle said. "As much as I hate to admit it, we need you. You can train us."

I studied their faces looking for signs of lying. "Aren't we living at the training center?"

"Yes, but there is no training going on since..." Ezra waved a hand over his legs.

"And Cheyenne died," Cory said, sitting up on the bed. "And the rest of the recruits disappeared."

"The rest?" I asked, my interest piqued.

Annabelle stood and paced back and forth. "Yeah,

don't you think it strange that this group home only has four teens?"

I did think that was strange. But I hadn't been here long enough to investigate or think about it. I'd been thrown into things pretty quickly, but there was no reason to say that. In the twenty minutes we still had before lunch I needed to find out everything I could about Brightwood and the three teens left behind.

"How many missions have you gone on?" I asked them.

Annabelle slammed a hand on my dresser. "One."

Cory and Ezra nodded their heads in agreement.

"Ezra wasn't supposed to be in the field at all," Cory explained while staring at Ezra's legs.

"So you guys have only been on one mission. Cheyenne was killed, which by the way, oh my gosh I'm so sorry. But then they ship all the other teens off somewhere else?"

Annabelle plopped back in the chair and hung her head back, her pink hair flopping with her. "Yep, that's right. And now Reggie has us go on 'missions' but they are glorified shopping trips or pretend recon."

"Until today," Ezra said. "We got these cards in our mailboxes. They gave us your trailer park as an address."

He handed me the card.

I took it and turned it over. Sure enough, my address was on the back.

"What was the objective?"

Ezra shifted in his chair. "There was none. Or at least we didn't have any instructions."

"Sometimes we get instructions at our first or second destination," Annabelle explained.

Cory sat up. "We used to."

I untangled my legs and stood up. "Guys, I don't think my godmother Joan was the only target."

I knew I was speculating, throwing spaghetti at the wall, hoping something stuck. But someone had *shot Joan.* Right in front of me. That wasn't nerves or imagination. That was a bullet and blood and chaos.

And Cheyenne—everyone kept saying she died on a mission. But the more I heard, the less it sounded like an accident. Like maybe no one was telling the whole story.

Maybe it was all just coincidence. Maybe I was spinning conspiracy theories because it was easier than sitting still. *But what if I wasn't wrong?* What if something was actually going on here—something no one wanted us to see?

The lunch gong sounded. I'd have to share my theories later. Probably better I didn't flesh them out now. Not until I knew who I could trust.

Without a word, we all slipped out to our own rooms to change into uniforms.

A few minutes later, we regrouped by the elevator.

"Don't forget after lunch we have counseling," Ezra reminded us.

"That's all we do anymore. Counseling, school work and grocery store shopping," Annabelle complained as she stepped on the elevator.

She punched the first floor button with more vigor than necessary and stomped a foot.

———

After a pretty quiet and uneventful lunch, I followed the other teens to the counseling room. Showing up at this meeting was for recon purposes only. I planned to share nothing about my past. Or my present. I'd never been to a group counseling session before. The only info I had on them, I'd gained by watching DVDs. Most likely not accurate.

"Hello, have a seat Cory, Ezra, Annabelle. And you must be Ellie. I'm Callum."

His salt-and-pepper hair was neatly combed. He smelled of antiseptic, and his gray eyes seemed to study me like he could see right through me. He wore a soft, brown cardigan over a white shirt, the sleeves rolled up, making him look more like some-one's favorite uncle than a counselor.

"Take a seat." He motioned to the small circle of

chairs. "Let's start with something easy. Ellie, why don't you introduce yourself to the group?"

I noticed he was holding his right bicep with his left arm and grimacing every other second. Either he was cold—which, no, it was definitely *not* cold in this room—or he was having a heart attack.

Or… he was injured.

Could this be the man I shot with an arrow?

My stomach tightened. Would he really be that bold? Just stroll into Brightwood like nothing happened? Was this some twisted coincidence, or was he part of something bigger? Something I was only beginning to see the edges of?

I didn't know. Not yet.

"Hi, I'm Ellie." I jumped up out of my seat and in three short steps I was in front of him. "I'm more of a hugger," I said, which I definitely was not. I was more of a stay-in-my-room-and-don't-talk-to-me type. But I had an agenda.

I pulled his good arm. I was guessing, and probably totally wrong, but a hug wouldn't hurt. Or it would. He stood and I embraced him in the biggest bear hug I'd ever done in my life.

He groaned and I stepped back as his white shirt was swallowed by a blob of crimson.

"Guys." I turned to the teen spies. "This is who I shot."

CHAPTER
SEVEN

THE ONE WITH THE DEAD COUNSELOR

COUNSELOR CALLUM GROANED.

"Ellie, what the heck?" Ezra said.

Callum stepped back and grasped a chair for support. "I just had surgery." He turned and staggered out into the hallway.

"I know you're going all *Hunger Games* on us," Annabelle said, "but you might at least ask us about Callum before you attack."

She was on her feet now and before I could do anything, she was in my face, pointing a finger at my chest. She jabbed it three times.

"Callum has been our counselor since…" Her voice trailed off, and her bottom lip quivered.

"She didn't know, Annabelle," Cory added.

"I'm sorry, I was just trying to help." I glanced at

Ezra, silently begging for backup. He dropped his head to his chest and crossed his arms.

I'd messed everything up.

The room reeked of the metallic scent of blood.

I looked down at my uniform. It wasn't the room. It was me.

My Brightwood uniform—plaid skirt, stiff white button-down, and navy blazer stamped with the school's emblem—was splattered with blotchy patches of black and red. Chick-fil-A cow spots, I thought absurdly. My brain was apparently still running comedy reels while the rest of me was unraveling. The white collar clung to my neck, sticky and cold. I'd changed after the woods, but no amount of clean clothes could scrub off what had happened. Or what I'd done.

I backed away from Annabelle, who was still inches from my face. "I'm sorry, guys."

Her lip had stopped trembling. Her eyebrows pinched into one straight, unforgiving line.

"You don't belong here," she spat.

I took that as my cue to exit. I sidestepped to avoid brushing against her and hurried out.

Tears blurred everything as I ran down the hallway toward the elevator. I couldn't stop the reel playing in my head. *How did I get here?* I should've stayed quiet at the trailer park, solved my mom's murder, and gone back to our off-the-grid life.

But what about Joan—

My thought cut off as I tripped over something solid and landed hard.

Right on top of Callum.

I gasped and pushed myself up on one arm, like a broken kickstand.

His face was the color of an eggplant.

A ragged breath scraped my throat as footsteps pounded behind me. The others were coming—I didn't have to look to feel them closing in.

Annabelle shrieked.

"Is he dead?" Cory asked.

I stood slowly, my now bloodstained skirt heavy around my knees. "Yes. Looks like a…" I swallowed. "Heart attack."

The elevator dinged.

Theo and Vivian stepped out to find four teens standing over a body. Me—drenched in blood, trembling, caught in the wreckage of another bad decision.

"Call 911!" Vivian shouted.

"He's gone," I said.

Theo pulled out a phone and dialed. Vivian eyed me with shock and suspicion.

Theo ushered us back into the common room and ordered us to sit down before joining Vivian in the hallway.

"See what happens when you don't do a thorough intake interview?" Theo spat, loud enough for us to hear.

"Keep your voice down. We don't know that she killed Callum," Vivian whispered, but it echoed down the hallway into the common room.

"She has blood on her uniform, and everyone knows Caroline went rogue. Like mother, like daughter."

Ezra's eyes grew wide at this last statement.

"Your mom went rogue? That explains a lot," Annabelle said as a tear dripped down her cheek. "You murdered Callum."

"I did not kill Callum," I said through gritted teeth.

"She didn't even know her mom was a spy until this morning," Ezra defended me. "Let's not forget she lost someone today too."

I smiled a quick wobbly smile at Ezra. He was on my side again.

"Ellie was right," Cory said. "That purplish look on Callum's face. That screams heart attack."

"Listen, I know I'm the new kid and everything's been a disaster since I got here, but let's be real—it's been a disaster long before me."

Ezra stared down at his legs. "She's not wrong."

I paced back and forth to help me process. "Okay. Just—let me say this again. You told me Brightwood's a training center for teen spies. Got it." I spun back toward them. "But how many were here before... all of this?"

"Thirty-four," Ezra said. "We were all being trained in our zone of genius, so to speak."

"And yours is computers and technology?"

"Yes."

"Annabelle?"

She wiped her eyes. "I don't know. I had just started when…" It was her turn to trail off.

I didn't ask Cory. It was evident he was the braun.

Cory stood and flexed his muscles. "Aren't you going to ask me?"

Despite the seriousness of the situation, I giggled. "Comic relief?" I suggested.

He flexed again. "Exactly."

"Guys, surely you realize Brightwood is under attack. Someone is trying to shut it down."

"So what are we supposed to do?" Annabelle whined. "We aren't trained like you. Not to mention, we don't have homes to go to."

I let the last comment go. I knew Annabelle was afraid. She'd been picked to be trained as a spy, but she didn't see her value. Instead, she attacked me with verbal jabs.

"I'll train you," I said.

Cory leapt over a chair. "Cool. Can you teach us some of the moves you used at the trailer park?

Annabelle stood."Can you teach me to blend in, like you did? Not an old woman, but something sexy."

"No, Annabelle, I think you're meant to stand

out. Not like you did this morning. I wouldn't advise standing in a field to draw the bullets of a sniper." I had to admit, Annabelle had guts but I wasn't going to tell her that. Not yet. I didn't want to give her false confidence. Her opinion of herself inflated too easily. It was better she stayed down to earth until she actually had some skills to be confident in.

Ezra had been silent during our impromptu there's-a-dead-body-in-the-hallway meeting. But this wasn't just any dead body. It was the counselor who'd helped him get over losing his legs and walk again—well, not helped him *get over* losing his legs, but at least function. Move forward. Exist.

"I'm in," Ezra said. "As long as we find out why our first mission failed and take whoever is responsible down." He stood and joined us in our semicircle, which we'd subconsciously formed. "But I stay in the van, so to speak."

I stuck my hand out. "Deal."

He reached out and shook it. This was not the time to be having romantic feelings, but there was no stopping the warmth creeping up my arm to my heart.

"Are we all in?" Cory asked.

"One more thing," I added. "Actually two. Get my mom out of prison, and take down the person responsible for Joan's death."

"Deal," they replied in unison.

The elevator creaked and rumbled, interrupting

what I thought would be a really cool pact we'd make with a handshake or something.

Boots echoed down the hallway to the doors of the counseling room. A squad of uniform-clad men with shields burst in as if they were entering a war zone, not a room with four teens.

A black-uniformed man grabbed my shoulders—clean-shaven, jaw tight, not a hair out of place. He smelled faintly of pine, like he'd been scrubbed for inspection. His eyes locked on mine, sharp and unblinking. No panic. No hesitation. Just controlled precision. His grip didn't waver as he spun me around and snapped the cuffs on with practiced ease.

"Ellie Quinn, you are coming with us."

PSYCH MEETS PRISON BREAK: TORTURE EDITION

JUST LIKE IN A MOVIE, one of the military-grade men threw a hood over my head and dragged me down the hallway toward the elevator. Instead of shrieking like Gus would have, I tried to be more like Shawn. My teammates — wait…did I just call them that? They'd gone from strangers to teammates in less than twenty-four hours.

As the men hauled me away, my teammates defended me.

Annabelle threatened, "You can't just take her."

"Yeah," Ezra interjected. "She didn't kill anyone."

"You mean murder. She didn't *murder* anyone," Cory said, extra emphasis on *murder* like he was auditioning for a courtroom drama.

The elevator doors clamped shut, slicing off the

rest of my team's commentary like a guillotine of awkward silence.

Why did he say that?

Murder. Not "accident." Not "incident" or "unfortunate cardiac event." He said it like it was a done deal.

But I didn't. I just… hugged him too hard.

Okay, that sounds ridiculous. I know it. But he'd gone still in my arms, not because I'm some secret assassin, but because his heart gave out. Right? *Right?*

The elevator hummed as it descended—smooth, sterile, way too quiet. My breath caught in my throat. I didn't know where we were going or who these men were, but I knew who they weren't: cops. They didn't walk like cops. Didn't talk like them either. They moved like ex-military, hired muscle, or the kind of guys who make people disappear in spy novels and government conspiracy thrillers.

And suddenly, I wasn't just wondering what Cory meant.

I was wondering who the *real* threat in this elevator might be.

The elevator blipped as we descended each floor. Why were we going down? And how far down did the basement go? Three blips. Three floors. Then I was in a tunnel of sorts. Not that I could see it, but I could smell damp musty air. The lights buzzed. We walked maybe forty steps—me half-dragged, half-aware—before the air changed. We were outside and I was shoved in the back of a van with a fresh new carpet smell.

Navigating in the van and paying attention would be a bit more difficult. I sat up and leaned against the hard plastic panel.

"Don't get any ideas," a gruff voice said. He followed up the command with a swift kick of his boot to my left calf. That was going to bruise.

What did he mean by "don't get any ideas"?

The worst he could do is kick me again. Or kill me. But I took the gamble and asked him. "What do you mean by 'any ideas'?"

"We've heard all about you," another low voice from the front of the van said.

"What have you heard?" I continued, tentatively. It was like walking a tight rope. One wrong question, or move for that matter, and it could mean the end for me. That is, if these were the same men who shot Joan. We hit a pothole in the road and my butt flew in the air and bounced on the carpet. I wished I'd studied the potholes more. What a ridiculous thought. Ridiculous, but true. An important detail.

"Let's just say we know about your skills with a bow," the man in the front said. Then he said nothing. I was alone with my thoughts even though there were other people in the van.

It was pointless to try to escape with two other men in the back with me. I knew there were two because of their breathing. Shallow. Controlled. Almost relaxed. I wasn't fooled. Shallow slow breathing was not only an intimidation trick, as if we are in control and you are not. The breathing technique was also conservation for action. The action these men would use wasn't something I wanted to test.

So I listened and tried to imagine the route we were taking. After sixty seconds, we hit the same pothole. I felt it in my tailbone the same way I had a minute earlier. Were we going around the block? After we'd hit the same bone-jarring pothole three more times, I knew I was right. We were driving around the block. My hypothesis was proved true when we parked and rough hands pulled me out of the van and back into the damp musty tunnel we'd come from less than five minutes ago.

A new theory slowly formed. Maybe this was a test. Maybe this was all part of the Brightwood initiation. Or training.

Once at the end of the tunnel, we didn't get on the elevator. They dragged me down a hallway and came to a full stop—probably in front of another door. I heard the subtle *beep-beep* of a keypad being punched. My head cover—it wasn't a sack, not quite. More like a blackout hood made of thick mesh-lined fabric, heavy enough to block out light and disorient you just enough to make you forget your own name— muffled the sound.

The second we were inside, someone ripped it off. My eyes flinched at the sudden overhead light. Bright, sterile. The kind of light meant for interrogation or surgery. Definitely not a friendly welcome committee.

I caught a blur of movement before the one with the gruff voice shoved me down into a chair.

"Now you will tell us everything you know."

His words came out sharp. Practiced.

I blinked, forcing my breathing to slow. My heart hadn't gotten the memo.

Everything I know?

About what? About Callum? About Brightwood?

Or about why my hands wouldn't stop shaking?

I didn't answer. Not yet. I was too busy scanning the room. No windows. One door. One fake window—definitely a two-way mirror. The walls weren't padded, so at least I wasn't in a psych ward. But there was a drain in the floor. Never a good sign.

Why did Cory say "murder"?

He must've meant Callum. The counselor.

The man I had technically hugged to death.

But then why did it sound like he meant something else?

"Everything I know about what?"

Good. Now I would have a chance to study all of them. Once I figured out who was in charge, I could play to him.

"Brightwood," one of them said as he shook my shoulders.

"Listen guys, you have this all wrong. I'm a foster kid. And Brightwood is a foster home. Yeah, a super posh one, but a foster home all the same."

They asked me a few more questions. Questions that basically asked the same thing. Just phrased differently.

"Why are you at Brightwood?"

"What do you do at Brightwood?"

I answered the best I could, repeating exactly what I'd said before. Not the truth, of course. Not that I'd watched my godmother take a bullet to the head, clean and precise. Not that I'd shot someone with my crossbow in the woods behind my trailer park. Not that the Brightwood counselor was already lying cold on a morgue slab.

While I gave nondescript answers and stared at them, taking note of every detail, their frustration level grew.

"We're going to have to up our interrogation," the gruff one said.

While they huddled a few feet away, whispering about what to do with me, I ran through the worst-case scenarios like flashcards I couldn't unsee. They'd made it inside Brightwood. That much was obvious. Which meant they'd found the hidden basement. The other basement. And the tunnel. If they had gotten that far, what else had they done? Shot Reggie? Taken out the maid? Tortured them for access codes or intel? Maybe Theo and Vivian were already dead. The thought punched the air from my lungs. If that was true—if *any* of that was true—I was alone. Completely alone. And so was the rest of my team.

Gruff Voice rejoined me and jerked me to my feet. "Time to find out what you really know."

He shoved me on a metal chair in the middle of the room, zip-tied me, and left. I could escape my bonds now. But where would I go? Surely he had locked the door. A voice crackled from the speakers in the wall.

"I think you'll tell us more in a minute."

Before he finished the word minute, a frigid shower of water drenched me and continued to increase in intensity. I gasped momentarily at the shock of the cold. Momentarily, because Mom had taught me to withstand the elements with training exercises. I'd acclimated to the cold waterfalls she'd made me stand under so much so that I showered in them in the summer.

I had to pretend. I continued to gasp, sputter, and thrash around.

Gruff Voice yelled, "Ready to talk yet?"

"Brightwood is a foster home," I sputtered. "I'm a foster kid."

When I repeated those answers, I knew something worse than water was coming. I hazarded a guess – loud music.

The room went dark and the music pulsed from the speakers and the water from the ceiling.

It wasn't the volume that got to me.

It was the way the song circled back on itself, like a snake eating its own tail—except louder, sharper, more synthetic. The beat thudded through the floor, rattling up my spine and into my teeth. The lyrics were nonsense—something about love and trust— but the delivery was mechanical and sticky, like syrup on a rusty speaker.

My ears rang. My bones hurt. My brain begged for stillness.

I tried to cover my ears, but the zip ties cut into my wrists, reminding me how trapped I really was. The walls pulsed with noise—low, guttural, vibrating through the concrete like some mechanical heartbeat. There was no off switch. No silence. No mercy. Just sound. Endless, pounding, inescapable sound.

Mom had once told me they used music as torture in places like black sites: "Volume, rhythm, repetition," she'd said, as casually as if she were teaching me how to braid my hair. "They use it because it doesn't leave marks. It worms into your thoughts. That's the point."

I remember blinking at her, maybe thirteen at the time, wondering why she knew that. She had just looked ahead at the road and said, "You don't need to block it out. You won't win that way. What you do is take it apart—turn the weapon into a puzzle."

Right now, I really wished I'd asked a follow-up question.

The song looped again, same stupid chorus. I could feel my grip slipping—not my hands, my *mind*. Like it wanted to turn to static just to match the noise.

So I fought back the only way I could.

I started rewriting the lyrics in my head.

"I love stew, you love peas,

Let's all eat moldy grilled cheese."

It didn't make sense. That wasn't the point. The point was—*they* didn't get to own the rhythm. I did. If I could rewrite it, I could survive it.

I kept going.

"I love tea, you love scones,

Somebody get me earplugs and a phone."

A laugh sputtered out of me: Dry. Ugly. But real.

I leaned my forehead against my knees and pictured the dining room at Brightwood. The long wooden table. The chandelier Ezra claimed was haunted. Cory arguing with Annabelle about whether soup counted as a beverage.

Room by room, memory by memory, I built my escape hatch. I walked the halls in my head. I heard the creak of the second stair. I saw the red mug in the kitchen, the one with the chip on the rim. I heard Mom's voice, low and firm in the back of my mind: *"Take it apart. Break it down. They don't get to break you."*

The music roared louder now. Maybe they turned it up. Maybe I was just losing my grip.

I clenched my fists, zip ties biting into my wrists, wishing I could cover my ears. Wishing I could make it stop.

But I knew one thing for sure: These men weren't stopping.

I had to escape.

CHAPTER
NINE

THE MUSIC SLICED OFF MID-SCREECH, leaving my ears ringing in a nauseating vacuum. Before I could savor the quiet, a woman's voice cracked through the speaker, crisp and furious.

"Who authorized this?"

No one answered. Even the walls seemed to hold their breath.

The hoses clicked off. Water streamed from my hair and soaked the concrete beneath my penny loafers. I blinked against the sting, shaking my head as far as the zip ties allowed—half dog, half drowned rat—trying to clear the waterlogged roar from my ears. My pulse thundered louder than the music had.

Great. Quiet is just a pause before the next round, I

told myself. *Stay upright. Stay conscious. Count every breath.*

I straightened my spine, droplets sliding down the back of my neck like icy fingers, and waited to see which voice—and which weapon—would come at me next.

"I repeat. Who authorized this?"

"It was me," another woman's voice answered.

Was that Joan? It couldn't be. I saw her die.

Someone must have shut the sound system down because for the next few minutes, I sat alone in silence. The only noise I heard was inside my head. My thoughts were loud, arguing – Joan can't be alive. I re-enacted the entire scenario. I saw the blood. The wound. I shot the sniper with a cross bow.

The door swung open like a scene from *every bad action movie ever*, and in walked a poster child for Tactical Weekly—biceps for days, uniform starched enough to cut glass.

Great. The for-hire military version of Buzz McNab.

He didn't say a word as he yanked off my restraints.

I stood, slow and shaky, then let my body collapse forward like a sack of potatoes.

If Shawn Spencer taught me anything, it's that playing unpredictable is half the game.

He flinched under my weight.

Point for Ellie. Zero for G.I. Joe.

I took a crazy chance for the second time today…I

righted myself and gave him a swift sucker punch to where the arrow I had shot would have landed. He reeled back and stumbled.

"What the heck, kid. I'm letting you go," the gruff voice.

"I shot you."

Then he did the most incredulous thing: He smiled and his square jaw smoothed out. He laughed and his eyes twinkled. "I didn't think you could do it. But you did."

"Did what?"

"Shoot me."

"So I'm right. What is going on here?"

He ignored my question and said, "I heard the other kids call you Katniss but I didn't believe it."

"Believe what?" This conversation was getting me nowhere. It was clear they were letting me go. Or were they? Was this another test? He shot Joan. I shot him. Maybe they had some computer thing to mimic Joan's voice so I would be fooled into thinking she was alive and they – whoever they were – were on my side.

Since Gruff Voice had no intention of telling me what was going on, I tried the direct approach. "Why did you kidnap me, drive me around the block for five minutes, and bring me back to Brightwood?"

"You're as badass as Joan said you were."

"You shot her!" I yelled, losing my patience.

"Nah, that was all staged." He straightened and

rolled his shoulders back, and a blob of blood seeped through the black uniform shirt where the arrow had pierced his chest. "Your arrow was not."

"Oh, why aren't you hurt worse…" I paused and answered for him. "Kevlar."

He shook his head in the affirmative.

"Could I have a towel?" I added as an afterthought.

"I'm sure we can find you one. Come meet the rest of the team."

He led me out the door and into the adjoining room where Joan sat next to Vivian. They froze mid-argument when I stepped in. It was as if someone had pushed the pause button on them.

Four men stood against a row of dusty, ancient computers—broad shoulders, buzz cuts, expressions carved from stone.

I mentally assigned them names:

Buzz — my new best friend with the bruised ego.

Lassiter — older, with a scowl that probably scared small children.

Gus — sharp-eyed and already judging me.

And **The Chief** — arms crossed, radiating "I'm in charge" vibes.

If this was a Psych episode, I was clearly the wildcard —and these guys weren't laughing.

"Look at her!" Vivian said as she rose from her seat, took off her cardigan, and threw it around my shoulders.

I shrugged the sweater off and jogged to Joan. I pulled her to her feet and wrapped my arms around her, squeezing all the air out of her. "You're not dead. I'm so glad you're not dead."

"Yes, sorry about that," she squeaked. "Can you let go, you're getting me all wet."

"That's just the beginning of the payback for making me think you were dead." I gave her one last squeeze before I let her go.

"I guess you are wondering what is going on here," she stated. She motioned to the chair that Vivian had vacated.

I sat and Gruff Voice handed me a towel. I took it and ran it over my hair, grabbing the moisture, stopping the annoying drip down my back.

"Yes, that would be nice."

"We haven't finished our conversation," Vivian interjected. "You don't have my permission to take my recruits off-book and torture them."

Joan stood and placed her hands on her hips in a super man pose. "Vivian, we aren't finished with our conversation. But this…" she motioned to the window of the room I'd been in. "Is exactly why your recruits aren't ready."

Note to self: *Never get in the middle of a Joan-Vivian showdown. Pretty sure this is how cities get leveled in superhero movies.*

"So today was a test."

"Yes," Joan answered.

Of course it was a test. Because normal interviews and personality quizzes are just too mainstream for Bright-wood. Next thing you know, they'll be asking me to defuse a bomb before breakfast.

She turned back to Vivian. "And if you would test the teens before you sent them to the field…"

Movement near the door caught my eye.

The scowling guy—Lassiter, as I'd dubbed him—checked his phone. His jaw tightened before he leaned toward The Chief and muttered something too low to catch.

The Chief gave a single nod, and Lassiter disappeared out the door without a word.

Great. First rule of spy school—when the grumpiest guy leaves mid-argument, it's never for coffee and donuts.

"Ezra's injury is not my fault." Vivian's face turned ten shades of red. The blue veins in her neck throbbed so hard I thought they were going to explode.

"What about Cheyenne?" Joan shot back.

"They were…" Vivian trailed off, gaze flicking away. The guilt in her eyes wasn't just a glimmer—it was a full confession.

"And what about the thirty recruits that are missing?" Joan's voice was like flint.

I didn't even pause before I spoke. "I thought they were moved to other foster homes."

The words felt hollow the second they left my mouth. Like saying it out loud would somehow make it true. But I didn't believe it—not really. Not after everything I'd seen.

"This isn't a foster home," Joan snapped, motioning to the cement cell I'd just escaped from and the wall of silent, armed muscle behind her. "Which I'm sure you've figured out by now."

She stalked across the room, boots echoing like gunshots, and jabbed her finger into Vivian's chest. "And she let her recruits be taken from right under her nose and didn't say a single word."

My brain was spinning like one of those corkboards with the red string—except all the strings led to question marks. Who took them? Was it punishment for Brightwood losing an agent? For Ezra? Were the powers-that-be trying to bury something—or someone?

And what if we were next?

"That's why you reactivated and placed me here," I said to myself more than anyone else. "So does that mean my mother really isn't in prison?"

Joan stepped back from Vivian, who froze with her mouth hanging open.

She turned to me with a sad smile. "No, I'm sorry that part is true."

My stomach dropped like I'd just missed the last step on a staircase.

So much for the hopeful your-life-is-a-lie twist where Mom was actually sipping lattes undercover.

Reality check: prison was still her address.

Vivian regained her composure and spoke to both of us. "Someone is targeting past and present agents."

"Like my mom," I added, the full weight of the situation sinking in. Being at Brightwood wasn't just about getting my mom out of prison, but also finding thirty missing agents. And possibly saving more.

A knock rattled the door before it even opened. One of the military guys—Lassiter — stepped in, his scowl deeper than before.

"We've got a problem."

Joan turned, already tense. "What now?"

He didn't flinch. "They know she's here."

His eyes landed on me, and my stomach flipped.

"Who's *they*?" I asked, though I already knew I wouldn't like the answer.

Lassiter's jaw clenched.

"The Alliance. And they're coming for you."

REDHEADS AND REBELS: A VERY BRIGHTWOOD BRIEFING

MY EYES DARTED between Vivian and Joan. "Who is The Alliance?"

"And you blame me?" Vivian's voice cut sharp and clear as she stepped forward, arms crossed like a shield. "You haven't even told her who she is. You promised she was the best—the one who could save Brightwood—and yet she doesn't even know what The Alliance is. You kept her in the dark and expect her to lead the charge?"

She turned on her heel and stormed out the door, leaving me with Joan, Gus, Lassiter, The Chief, and Buzz. My kidnappers were staring at me in that is-she-really-   the-person-who-is-supposed-to-save-us way. Everyone except Buzz, who patted his sore chest with a look of pride.

I'm pretty sure I looked like a drowned, scraggly, red-haired rat. I had none of the bulk these men and Cory had. None of the tech skills Ezra possessed. None of the stand-out-like-you-mean-it confidence Annabelle had perfected. Mom had taught me to blend in, not be seen. Sure, I'd perfected Shawn's "go boneless" move (you know, the one he uses to flop limply when Gus shoves him around), and I could recite every obscure line from the show, but could I actually save Brightwood? I didn't know what or who The Alliance was, but I wasn't the girl for the job.

The Chief motioned for his men to follow him. They marched out the door in a military-like procession, leaving Joan and me alone.

So many emotions and questions swirled around in me: I was angry with Joan for faking her assassination. Relieved she was alive. Astounded that she thought I was the agent to save Brightwood. I didn't feel like an agent. Just a girl who could shoot a crossbow and live off the grid.

"Well," I said, finally breaking the silence.

She crossed her arms and leaned back on a table that housed a bank of monitors. "Well, what?"

"Why did you fake your assassination? Why did you have me kidnapped and tortured? Who is The Alliance? And last but certainly not least — why did you tell these people I could save Brightwood?"

"Are you finished?"

"No. I have more questions. But those will do for a start."

"I'll answer your questions, but not right this minute. We have a briefing with the team in ten minutes. Go get ready."

"I can just go?"

"Yes," she handed me a keycard. "Use this to operate the elevator. Go up to your room and get cleaned up."

"What's to stop me from walking out the front door?"

"Nothing."

"So I can leave."

"Absolutely. But you won't."

"Why won't I?"

"You want your mom out of prison. And whether you want to admit it or not, you want to save Brightwood and take down The Alliance, or at least find those thirty teens."

"How do you know that?"

"I've known you all your life. You've been trained all your life for something like this."

"So I'm just a tool to be used and manipulated." I was being harsh and I knew it.

"No. Your Mom got out of the spy game for you. But there is one thing she couldn't do."

"What's that?"

"Get the spy out of you." She shrugged and

pulled me into her arms once more. "Think about that one."

She released me and left. I stared at the room for a moment before exiting and hopping on the elevator.

———

Five minutes later, I'd changed into the uniform that had been laid out on my bed. There was a loud rap on the door.

"Ellie, let's go to the briefing together!" Cory's loud boisterous voice cajoled.

I opened the door. Annabelle grinned at me, practically bouncing with energy. She wore the uniform too—but she'd glammed it up with a glittery pink scarf and belt. Her hair was tied into two knots on top of her head, like fuchsia drawer knobs. Cory stood just behind her, smirking like this was all perfectly normal.

"You're not going to the briefing like that are you?"

"What's wrong with this?" I smoothed the plaid skirt.

"Listen girl, if you can put all that effort into looking eighty-five, the least you can do is let that fiery hair work for you."

Before I could say a word, she pulled a comb from her pocket and worked her Annabelle magic on my hair. Next, she pulled out her phone and snapped a photo and showed me. By magic, I mean I had two fiery red knobs on my head, fraternal twins to hers.

Cory slouched on the door frame, his eyes scanning my room.

"You travel light, Katniss. You should have seen Annabelle's load of suitcases when she got here."

Annabelle turned and punched him in the arm which resulted in an "OUCH" from her instead of him.

"Where's Ezra?" I hoped they weren't going to say he dropped out because today was too much for him. Joan may think that she was right about me staying because the spy was in me. She was right that I wanted to free my mom from prison. But there was another reason I wanted to stay. Another person I wanted to stay for: Ezra. I felt my face flush.

"He's running the tech for the meeting, silly," Annabelle said as she linked arms with me. "Let's go."

Something was bothering me as I tromped down the stairs behind Cory and Annabelle. At first, I couldn't put my finger on it—just a low buzz of wrongness humming in my chest. I replayed the chaos from earlier: the paramedics, the way no one would meet my eyes. Had I missed something? Something I should've noticed but hadn't? A pulse? A gasp? A sign he might still be alive and wheeled off to some off-the-books hospital room where they could finish what I'd started?Then it hit me: *Was Callum really dead?*

I made a dead stop that broke the Annabelle–Ellie walking chain.

"Is Callum dead?"

"Yes," Cory said, not even looking back.

"Why aren't you two more upset?"

"Oh, we are," Annabelle replied with a grin. "We're going to get the best anecdote for grief."

"A funeral?" I asked.

"No," Cory answered. "Revenge."

"Oh!" My mouth stayed in an 'o' for a few more seconds.

"Don't worry, Els, we're not going off-book," Cory added.

For some reason, I doubted he was telling the truth.

Maybe it wasn't just grief. Maybe Callum knew the mission was doomed before it started. Maybe he'd carried the guilt of losing Cheyenne and Ezra like bricks strapped to his chest—until his heart just gave out. Or maybe it wasn't guilt at all. Maybe it was the weight of thirty missing recruits, gone without a trace, ripped away under his watch.

And maybe this wasn't about honoring Callum.

Maybe it was about punishing the people who broke him.

Annabelle and Cory led me to a room I hadn't been in yet. Similar to the computer bank adjacent to the torture room, but more high tech and cleaner. Ezra sat at the middle of a half circle table with a keyboard. He smiled and motioned to the seat next to him. Before I could pull it out, Theo and Vivian took the seats on either side of him. Where had they come from? The wall? In this house, that was entirely possible. I'd investigate the wall later. Wait, why did I want to investigate? Did that mean I was staying *again? How many times would I wrestle with my place here?* Staying to get my mom out of prison was entirely different than saving Brightwood and a lot more dangerous.

I decided to wait until the briefing was over before I committed to saving Brightwood. Joan, Gus, Lassiter, The Chief, and Buzz filed in. It was then I realized the rest of my team had seated themselves. I scrambled for one of the two remaining seats. The wheeled chair slid out from under me and I hit the cement floor with a thud.

"Sorry." I kneeled, and with some effort, rose to my feet.

If this was a welcome party, someone forgot the snacks. And the *welcoming* part.

I sat at the sleek half-circle table —facing a wall of screens big enough to make any conspiracy theorist weep with joy. Joan stood at the front, all business, while Vivian hovered nearby like a general waiting to deploy troops.

And speaking of troops...

Leaning against the back wall, arms crossed and faces carved from stone, were the four military guys who'd *"kidnapped"* me earlier. Or as I liked to call them—The Chief, Gus, Lassiter, and Buzz. Not their real names, obviously, but when you're thrown into a spy training op without warning, you cope by assigning names from your limited pop culture knowledge. Thanks, *Psych* reruns on DVD.

The Chief—gray hair, no nonsense—gave me a nod. I think that was his version of a smile. Or indigestion. Hard to tell.

Ezra sat at a control panel in front of the screens, fingers flying across a keyboard like he was born attached to it. I had no idea how he made those images appear—probably magic. Or Wi-Fi — whatever that was.

The screen blinked to life, revealing a logo of an eagle gripping a banner. It didn't take a genius—or a girl raised in the woods—to know this wasn't the friendly kind of bird.

Ezra quipped, "And now, for your viewing discomfort—America's Future."

Joan didn't acknowledge his humor. I was starting to think she had a 'no jokes during global crisis' policy.

"This organization," Joan began, her voice steady and sharp, "was dismantled two years ago. Or so we thought."

I recognized the name. *America's Future.* I'd heard

it in snippets—late-night conversations between Mom and Joan back when I pretended to be asleep. I didn't know the details, just that when it was 'taken down,' Mom hugged me tighter that night.

Ezra tapped a key, and the eagle morphed into something worse—a globe wrapped in heavy chains.

"This," Joan said, "is The Alliance."

A chill ran down my spine. Globes and chains weren't exactly subtle.

"The Alliance took what America's Future started and expanded it. Global reach. More resources. No borders. No conscience."

Cory let out a low whistle beside me. "Upgrading from national to international evil. Impressive."

I glanced at him—and caught the faint glow of his phone under the table as he typed something with his thumb. Casual — too casual.

Ezra pulled up a video feed—grainy footage of teens being marched through sterile hallways. No sound, but you didn't need audio to hear the fear.

Joan's voice softened, but it didn't lose its edge. "Thirty Brightwood agents. Taken. We believe they're being held in the reactivated facility beneath the Capitol—the same underground complex America's Future once used."

I didn't realize I was holding my breath until Annabelle shifted beside me. Ezra's usual smirk faded as he watched the footage.

Joan clicked to a new screen—this time displaying

a page from a handbook. The words practically shouted off the page:

We denounce Christianity.

We affirm the right to choose any lifestyle, any relationship, at any age.

We reject governments interfering with personal freedoms.

My stomach twisted. I didn't need a degree—or, you know, any formal education beyond what Mom taught me—to see this wasn't about freedom. This was about erasing anything that stood in their way.

Cory, still scrolling on his phone like he was Shawn Spencer pretending to Google something while secretly solving a case with zero actual research, chimed in. "Sounds like they're just cutting the red tape. Letting people live how they want."

I narrowed my eyes but kept my mouth shut. *File that under: Things to Worry About Later.*

Joan's gaze swept over us like she could see straight through to our thoughts. "The Alliance isn't offering choice—they're manufacturing obedience. Strip away identity, faith, and family, and you're left with perfect, compliant soldiers."

Ezra brought up a map dotted with red lights. "Alliance activity spans twelve countries. But their stronghold remains here. The Capitol tunnels weren't sealed like we believed."

Vivian finally stepped forward, pointing to a blinking section on the map.

Tactical mode: ACTIVATED blipped in bold, blocky letters.

"Our first move is infiltration. There's a secondary tunnel system—access point here." She tapped like she was ordering from a menu, not planning a break-in. "Small team. Stealth. Locate the agents. Extract intel."

Annabelle raised a brow. "And if extraction isn't an option?"

Vivian didn't hesitate. "Then we adapt."

Easy for her to say. I was still figuring out how to *log into life* outside the woods.

Joan's attention landed squarely on me. Again.

"Ellie," she said, voice lowering just enough to make it personal. "You were raised off the grid, but you've been training for this your whole life. Even when your mother walked away, you didn't stop. Because you were *born* for this."

Theo, lounging at the edge of the room like a discount motivational speaker, added with a smirk, "It's a lot for a rookie. No shame in sitting this one out."

I met his gaze with the same look I used to give raccoons trying to steal our food—*Try me, and you'll regret it.*

I glanced back at the screens—the stolen teens, the manifesto of madness, the map lighting up like a Christmas tree from the depths of dystopia.

Joan was right. I hadn't asked for this. But when

the world hands you a front-row seat to evil, you either look away—or you stand up.

So I stood. My voice didn't shake, even if my insides were doing somersaults.

"Guess it's time I find out what I was born for."

Ezra grinned like I'd just joined the cool kids' club. Annabelle gave a small approving nod.

Cory? Still typing. Still smirking.

The Chief and his crew straightened slightly, like they were already assessing whether I'd survive the next phase. All of them except Buzz, who patted his chest and saluted me.

Joan's lips twitched—almost a smile, but not quite.

"Good," she said. "We leave at dawn."

Of course we did. Because why storm an underground lair at a reasonable hour when you could do it sleep-deprived and questioning your life choices?

Note to self: Learn how to use a laptop. And maybe a cell phone.

And just like that, my *first day on the job I never wanted* officially got a whole lot more complicated.

CHAPTER
ELEVEN

PSYCH MEETS THE AVENGERS: ELITE AGENT EDITION

I AWOKE the next morning to the sun shining in the window.I climbed out of bed and checked my digital clock. Eight a.m. Something was wrong. Wait, what happened to the mission at the crack of dawn? Either I had missed the van or they had left me behind.

"You're awake." Annabelle barged in and plopped onto my bed like it was hers.

I turned from the window. "Did you steal my keycard?"

She grinned and waved it. "It was on your dresser. I'm calling it a tactical acquisition."

I sighed and rejoined her on the bed. "Did I miss a briefing?"

"No. Just breakfast. Theo told us then—mission's cancelled. Said we're not ready."

So I had missed breakfast.

"Vivian said to let you sleep in since you were tortured yesterday," Ezra added from the doorway, casually leaning against the frame. Apparently Annabelle had left the door wide open.

I was suddenly self conscious. I ran my hands through my hair and hoped I didn't look like death warmed over. I probably resembled something the forest spit out—half-alive, fully annoyed.

"Joan is here. She has a few expert agents coming to train us. Kat Gains and Adelina Hunter" he said, all casual.

Annabelle jumped up. "How can you report that so casually? You're kidding me. I'm freaking out here."

Ezra smirked. "I'd be more excited if they brought Maryanne, their tech genius"

I pulled the blanket over my head.

"Wake me when we're storming secret tunnels."

Annabelle whipped the blanket off my head. "Aren't you excited?"

I got a quick glance in the mirror. The static from the blanket caused my hair to stand on end. I smoothed it the best I could and swung my legs over the side of the bed. Ezra sank into the velvet armchair—the kind of chair that probably had a trust fund.

Cory swaggered in and leaned against the dresser as if he were posing for a model photoshoot. "Did you guys hear? Kat and Jim Gains. Adelina and Nathaniel Jones. They're all coming here. I'm pretty psyched man!" He thumped the DVD player on the dresser for emphasis and it cracked. "Wow, sorry Ellie, I don't know my own strength."

I was on my feet now, ignoring the apology and the broken DVD player for the moment. "I don't get it. You guys are more excited about celebrity agents than rescuing the thirty teens and taking down The Alliance?"

Annabelle stood and joined Cory at the dresser, smoothing her hair in the mirror. She reached into her holographic makeup pouch—one that looked like it had been stolen from a unicorn rave—and pulled out a lip gloss, applying it like she had an audience.

"Ellie has been so off-the-grid she doesn't know who the most powerful agents in the world are—"

Cory interrupted with, "Yeah, Jim Gains and Nathaniel Jones, like that can't be his real name. Gotta be an alias. This is so stinking cool."

Annabelle turned on him, "I meant females. Kat and Adelina."

"You guys are right. I've been off the grid so long, and didn't know until yesterday that I was an agent in training, so no I don't know who those people are."

The truth was I'd heard Kat and Jim's names.

When Joan and my mom had had late night conver-sations about America's Future being dismantled. Kat and Jim had taken them down. Jim had been shot and almost died. I didn't want to share that informa-tion right now. As much as I had wrestled internally with being an actual agent, right now I wanted to be one. Out there in the field in a secret underground tunnel, rescuing the thirty teens and taking down The Alliance, not listening to other agents drone on about their exploits.

"Okay, Katniss," Annabelle said. "You're about to meet them. We have a new briefing at nine." She waved her hand at the boys. "So clear out so I can get her dressed."

"I can dress myself," I retorted a little too harshly.

Ezra paused in the doorway. "I'll find you another DVD player." And then he was gone.

I guess Annabelle wasn't getting the hint, evidenced by the fact that she was pulling a fresh uniform out of the closet.

"Let's get you ready. I see the way you keep eyeing Ezra and fluttering those perfect eyelashes."

"What? I..."

If Annabelle saw it, did Ezra? Did everyone else? I'd have to be more careful with my eyelashes and with whatever other signals I was sending him. I had no training for boy-girl relationships. I could drop a turkey at thirty yards, easy. But put me in a room with a boy, and I was useless.

What I couldn't figure out was how to navigate a relationship with a guy I liked. *Liked? Where did that come from? Stop it. Stay on mission.* Free the thirty Brightwood Agents. Free mom from jail. Take down The Alliance.

"There's no denying it." She thrust the hanger toward me and pointed to the bathroom. "Go put this on and I'll take care of the rest."

I had a feeling "the rest" meant lots of makeup and another set of red knobs on top of my head. Neither of which I thought would help me with Ezra.

I'd somehow convinced Annabelle that less is more in the makeup department today. "These agents might make us run drills or something and I don't want this stuff running down my neck."

"Good point." She pulled a makeup wipe out of her pouch and removed the thick layer. "How about some mascara and lip gloss."

"Perfect." I surveyed myself in the mirror. The knobs on my head didn't look too awful.

Annabelle pumped a fist in the air. "Let's go meet some of the most famous agents on the planet!"

I paused in the doorway, surveying the room. Annabelle gave me a shove and I stumbled in and froze. Reggie stood at the front of the briefing room, Joan next to him. The Chief, Buzz, Lassiter, and Gus stood at attention at the back of the room. Ezra sat, once again, in the middle of the semicircle. I wouldn't make the mistake of trying to sit next to him again.

"Ellie, take a seat," Joan said, her voice laced with that special kind of exasperation she seemed to reserve just for me.

I kept my expression neutral—Mom's Rule #1: *Blend in so well they forget you're there.* So, I did exactly that. No eye rolls. No sighs. Just smooth, controlled movement as I slipped into the chair like I'd been trained for this my whole life.

Which I hadn't.

Because while Mom had taught me how to track a deer through dense forest and disappear without a trace, she'd skipped the "briefing room etiquette" lessons. Apparently, knowing when to nod seriously wasn't high on the survival checklist.

The only frame of reference I had was binge-watching *Psych* on scratched DVDs. And something told me that channeling Shawn Spencer's energy in a room full of military operatives—including the one I'd already nicknamed Lassie—wasn't exactly the fast track to spy of the year.

I folded my hands neatly in my lap, the picture of quiet compliance.

Shawn would've kicked open the door, declared himself psychic, and demanded a pineapple centerpiece by now.

I didn't even twitch.

Because while my brain was quoting Gus—*"I've heard it both ways"*—my body was following the real family motto:

Be invisible. Stay unnoticed. Watch everything.

And judging by Joan's lingering glance, she wasn't buying my act.

I turned and faced the front of the room when Reggie cleared his throat. "Team, as dwindled as we are, it's our job to get our fellow agents back."

I couldn't wrap my mind around this version of Reggie. I mean, I knew he was in charge of Brightwood, but he'd shown up at the front door as a butler. I'd only seen him act as a butler. Now he wore a charcoal slim fitted suit as if he were in front of a board room, not a group of misfit spies and four military spec guys.

"And because we are dwindled," Joan said, waving her arm toward the door as if she were on a game show. "We've brought in help."

As if in cue, the tallest, gangliest redheaded male I'd ever seen entered the door behind us. He wore khakis and a white button and looked the least agent-y I'd ever seen. He was followed by a brunette wearing a cardigan and trouser jeans. Maybe this was what Mom had been talking about — blend in so you don't stand out.

"Jim and Kat Gains, team." He motioned them to the front of the room and all eyes followed. "These two took down America's Future."

And yet, like a giant pimple you thought was gone, it popped back up again.

"Thank you, Reggie." Jim slapped Reggie on the back with a pumpkin-sized hand and sent him reeling forward. "Happy to help. We're disappointed that America's Future has had some sort of rebirth, but we've seen this happen before."

Annabelle shot out of her seat."With the New Reich?" she shouted.

A voice behind us said, "Yes, you're exactly right. Sorry we are late. Our kiddos, Sawyer and Payton, are going through a bit of separation anxiety."

I turned and couldn't believe my eyes. An older version of me. Her vibrant red hair matched mine. As she passed, she grinned at me and I gave her a quick goofy grin and wave. Her blue eyes matched mine in intensity.

Behind her, bringing up the rear, was a dark-skinned, chocolate-eyed man. It must be her husband, Nathaniel.

"Team, this is Adelina and Nathaniel Jones. And Annabelle is right. They took down the New Reich which was another world-wide organization that sprung up from a smaller trafficking ring in Poland. But I'll let them fill you in."

Maybe I didn't fit in here at all. I needed someone to fill me in. A giant three-ring binder with the info on these two couples would be helpful. I glanced around the room. It didn't look like anyone had paper of any kind. It was then that I got a great idea: I needed access to a computer with information and access to files. Ezra was the computer whiz. I could ask him. Spend time with him, catch up on America's Future and The New Reich, and learn about the agents helping us.

Once all of them were in the front of the room, Reggie handed the podium over to Jim, who was too tall for it. Nathaniel jumped in and fiddled with it, raising it to fit Jim. Sort of. Jim still had to lean over, which he did, casually placing both elbows on the top and addressing us as if we were a book club, not a group of spies.

"Shall we wait for the rest of the team before we start?" Kat addressed Jim from the position she'd taken beside Adelina and Nathaniel. Seconds before, Adelina and Kat had whispered to each other about kiddos and childcare.

"The rest of the team?" Joan asked, a perplexed look on her face.

Jim responded, "Yes. Damica, who is our profiler, and Maryanne, our tech whiz."

When Jim said the words "tech whiz" Ezra raised both hands in the air and cheered, "YES!"

"I didn't realize you were directing the briefing, Ezra," Reggie teased.

"I'm sorry, I'm just so excited Maryanne is going to be here. Do you know she was able to hack a network and talk to Damica when she went undercover with America's Future? I love her, man."

During his little speech, I'd turned and watched his face and the door at the same time. Another teen with blonde hair entered. By her youthful appearance, including a freckled face and hair topped by a beanie, I'd guess she was seventeen or eighteen at the most.

A goddess-looking woman followed her, with chestnut curls tipped with copper as if her hair had been dipped in gold. The tailored pink suit she wore could not hide the fact that she had long lean muscles and had spent a lifetime on keeping them that way. Of all the agent helpers, she stood out. Why wasn't she up at the podium? She radiated a glow that no one else in the room could measure up to.

When she walked behind Ezra's chair, Annabelle raised her foot and gave it a swift kick. She whispered, "She's right behind you."

"And she heard me say…"

"Yes, I heard you," Maryanne said. "And thank you, young man, but I'm spoken for." She giggled and raised her left hand showing a sparkly diamond.

"We're all here now," Jim said. "Let's get started. This is Maryanne and Damica ."

Annabelle thumped Ezra's chair again. He held the remote clicker in his hand and he froze. Ezra only had eyes for Maryanne.

Jim squinted at Ezra's lanyard, lips twitching as

he sounded it out. "Ezra," he said, then added impatiently, "Start the presentation."

"Oh." He fumbled the remote and it fell on the floor.

"How about I help him today? Mind if I sit next to you?" Maryanne asked as she motioned for the person sitting next to him to move.

The person sitting next to him was me. After all the I-don't-know-where-to-sit moments when I entered the room. After my mini-mental breakdown and stare off with Joan, I'd picked the seat next to Ezra. No, it had picked me. It had called me. And now I was giving it up to the person he really loved. Maryanne.

"As I was saying, we thought of sending a teen in to infiltrate The Alliance's secret training," Kat said.

"Not so secret," Damica added.

I shook my head, waking myself. I'd missed most of the meeting. I zoned out, mostly because I didn't know what was going on. I didn't have the knowledge about the organizations and agents the rest of the team did. My plan for asking Ezra to show me evaporated into a puff of Maryanne's perfume.

I'd moved to the back of the room and leaned up against the back wall with Lassiter on my right. When I woke from my information overload zoning to the statement "send a teen in to infiltrate The Alliance's secret training center," I jabbed an elbow into Lassie's side. I'm pretty sure that wasn't briefing room etiquette, but I needed to act fast.

"Didn't you say The Alliance is coming for me?"

"Yes, I told Vivian we should keep you under lock and key until the danger passes."

I ignored his comment and raised my hand up in the air, and in Shawn Spencer-style, I yelled, "Pick me!"

PSYCH MEETS HOMELAND: SPY CAMP BAPTISM BY POOL

I CAUGHT Kat and Adelina's attention with the "pick me."

Joan stood and crossed her arms. "We don't let our teen agents get kidnapped or taken."

I jabbed Lassiter again.

"Tell them what you told me," I hissed. "About The Alliance. And they're coming for you. That's what you said," I added, loudly enough for the whole room to hear.

"I repeat, we don't use our agents as bait."

Annabelle rose to her feet and pointed at the guest agents at the front of the room. "Maybe you don't but *they* do." Then she turned to Ezra. "Come on Ezra, back me up. You know it is true."

Ezra did a quick sideways glance at the girl he loved, Maryanne.

"It is true," she said. Ezra froze with a stupid grin on his face.

Her response was to grab the laptop. "Permission to take over for a moment, Jim?"

Jim ran a hand over his face and slumped forward on the podium. "It is true. However, it is unorthodox and highly dangerous." He stepped back and waved Kat and Adelina forward while he and Nathaniel took a place on the side wall.

"I was fifteen when I joined the Internal Task Force For Safe Children (ITFFSC)." Adelina started. A photo of Adelina looking frightened and young flitted across the screen. "At least these teens have some training. And she," she pointed at me. "She's been training her whole life."

I knew what I said next was going to be a stupid question because everyone else in the room knew who these celebrity-type agents were and what they'd done. At least I assumed they knew.

"What did you do first when you joined ITFFSC?"

"I was the bait. I let myself be trafficked by this man."

A handsome man with blonde hair and blued eyes flashed across the screen. He looked like someone you would trust if you needed directions. "This is Ryszard. He ran a trafficking organization in Poland that served as an international hub."

Another picture of a blonde model-type fair skinned, blue eyed girl replaced Ryszard's. "This is Daria. She was my best friend in the orphanage in Poland. He scouted her and trafficked her."

"So you had to *find* her and bring her *home*." I put emphasis on "find" and "home" to speak to Joan.

"Sorry I'm late." A long lean man in a priest's collar entered.

"We're not dead yet," Annabelle said, followed by a nervous laugh.

"Oh, this is Father Raphael. He's on the task force." Adelina explained. "We were just telling the team about my being the bait and letting myself be trafficked."

"This is the team?" He froze and took a visual sweep of the room.

Maryanne stood and put her hands on her hips. "You didn't read the file I sent you, did you?"

Kat nudged Adelina, who stepped forward, motioned toward me, and took the podium for the first time. "We have the perfect spy for this mission."

She paused. "There are thirty teen agents missing."

His gaze bored through me. "And this is who you plan to send in as bait."

"Yes," I said. "I offered."

"Just like you Adelina," Father Raphael said. "Please continue Kat, don't let my moral compass interrupt you."

Kat nodded to Maryanne. Maryanne clacked away on the computer and a picture of Kat appeared, looking similar to what she looked like right now, but more mousy.

"I let Devon, a man who was a foster kid in the Green Pines group home, kidnap me. His bio mother was feeding teens who were aging out of the system to him. He was trafficking them." When Kat began speaking, her mousy shell disappeared. She was the opposite of a turtle– when her true self poked out, she was confident and powerful.

Cory tapped the table impatiently. "I thought we were here to talk about America's Future and The Alliance."

Damica popped out of her seat. "I'm the one who went undercover with America's Future. That's why I'm here. I know all about the underground training facility because I was there." She sat down and added, "Oh and to profile each and everyone of you."

"What are you, like, 17?" Annabelle asked.

"I'm in my late thirties."

"Very late," Kat said with a grin.

"Don't you get it?" Kat continued. "The super-power of being an agent and going undercover is not looking like one. I'm just a timid librarian. No one would give me a second thought."

I repeated my mom's mantra: *"Blend in so you don't stand out."*

"That's right," Kat said. She waved an arm around the room. "Do any of us look like an agent?" She stopped at Maryanne. "Except Maryanne. And that's exactly why she's the tech girl."

"Not only that but she is a genius," Ezra added, complete with a goofy grin.

Kat ignored Ezra's comment and turned to Reggie. "So what do you say Reggie? Put Ellie in the field?"

"She's my agent," Joan interjected.

"Your agent which you kept hidden in a trailer park."

"Yes, and you let her think you'd been assassinated right in front of her," Vivian said, stepping into the room like a storm in heels. "And tortured her without mine or Reggie's permission."

"Yes, let's put her in the field," Reggie answered. "But can we have some intense training with your team, Jim?"

"Absolutely," Jim said. "That's what we are here for."

"I'd like to start profiling the agents," Damica interjected." We need to know what their weaknesses and strengths are."

Cory stood and flexed. "I'm the muscle."

Pride, I thought.

"And I'm the beauty."

Vanity.

"I'm the tech guy." Ezra raised both hands in the air.

Skill and blue eyes.

"And you?" Damica asked. "While you are all profiling yourselves."

"I'm pretty good with a bow and arrow. But not much else."

"And that is exactly why Ellie is ready to go into the field," Reggie said. "Its this little trait we call humility."

"While humility is important, so is knowing your strengths and weaknesses," Damica added. "We'll address both in your sessions."

The room was getting crowded. And although we had an idea of what we were doing next, I wanted tangible steps. An actual plan.

"Jim?" Kat waved her husband back up to the podium. As if she read my mind, she stated, "This is where you come in. Planning is your strength."

"Right. Ezra, if you can take over?" Jim gestured, and Maryanne slid the laptop back to Ezra with a sparkly smile.

After a few keystrokes, a calendar appeared, projected onto the screens behind them. Each of our names was color-coded. I was green.

Green for go?

Green for gross?

Or green like *you're about to sprint for your life, so maybe wear tennis shoes next time?*

Psych had never covered "briefing color psychology," but I was pretty sure it wasn't good.

"After I go over the schedule, I'll send it to your phones," Jim said, turning to the group.

I raised my hand. "I don't have a phone."

"She only knows how to use a DVD player. Nothing more technologically advanced," Annabelle supplied with a chuckle, slapping her knee like she'd just delivered the joke of the century.

As everyone laughed, I caught movement out of the corner of my eye.

Cory, head ducked low, was already tapping furiously on his phone—way too fast for someone just checking a schedule that hadn't been sent yet.

I tucked that little detail away in the back of my mind, where all the weird things went to marinate.

"Ezra, can you get Ellie a phone?" Jim paused as Ezra fished around in his bag.

"I meant to give it to you before the briefing." He stuck his hand containing the phone in my direction without turning to look at where I was. He dropped it and I caught it in midair.

I stared at the black screen. I didn't know what to do with it.

"Turn it on," Joan commanded from the side of the room.

Thanks, Joan. I fiddled with it, turning it over and over before she joined me at the back of the room and took it from me.

"You and Mom maybe should have covered phones and basic computer skills," I hissed.

Joan took the phone and swiped her finger up the screen. The word "hello" popped up and she shoved it in my hand.

"Put your face up to it."

I listened and it opened up a small computer looking screen. She tapped the file labeled schedule and it opened.

I studied the green, not only because I wanted to know my schedule but also because – to put it mildly- could I be any more humiliated? I tried to think about how Shawn and Gus handled humiliation. I couldn't exactly put a hand to my head and start shaking and then give a fake psychic reading. Could I?

Before I could decide my next move, Annabelle stood and hit the table with a fist. She turned and pointed to me. "She's in charge of training?"

I wondered where this bizarre twist had come from. Hadn't she asked me to train her? "She doesn't even know how to use a phone."

"You don't have to know how to use a phone to kill someone with a bow and arrow," I shot back, which was uncharacteristic of me. I was usually the one who followed along and did what I was told. The only problem with doing what I was told my whole life was no one had ever told me I was being trained to be a spy. Now all I wanted to do was get the teens back, get my mother out of prison, and get out of here for good.

"Girls, take a seat," Jim commanded.

Since I was sitting, I leaned back against the wall and crossed my arms.

"I think these two will work together well," Damica said as she punched Kat in the arm. "They remind me of us when we started."

Jim began speaking again, and once again I zoned out. I put my phone in my pocket after giving the schedule a quick read through. I wasn't *really* in charge of training. Annabelle was being dramatic. I was in charge of two sessions of weapons training: knife and bow. Probably more outdoor survival than weapons. And not needed for storming or infiltrating an underground training facility under the capitol building. More like let the girl who has trained her whole life at least feel like she fits in. Which I didn't.

When the meeting ended, I left before everyone stood and before Jim finished the last word in his sentence "group training starts at —" I had the schedule, right?

I didn't go to my room. Every time I went there, the rest of the teens showed up. I opted for a set of stairs. Hopefully, they would lead to a quick exit. Outside. I pushed on the first door I found. Glorious sunshine.

The pool glimmered invitingly in front of me. I didn't want to go inside and change. Surely there were bathing suits in the pool house. The pool house door was unlocked. I stepped in and found a set of lockers. One had my name on it. I opened it, found a dark green suit, goggles and flippers. I slipped into a curtained changing room and within a minute, I had the suit on and my uniform folded and placed in the locker with "Ellie" on it. I grabbed a towel off the shelf and stepped out of the pool house.

Good. No one had followed me so far. I set the towel down on a chaise lounge, placed the flippers by the side of the pool, stretched the goggles onto my head, and dove it. Much warmer than the rivers and lakes I was used to swimming in. I shoved my feet into the flippers, took a deep breath, took a dolphin-like dive and swam the length of the pool in one breath. I did the same five more times while I processed.

I've been trained to be an agent my whole life.

I knew I'd thought about that plenty last night while I tossed and turned in my sweat-soaked sheets, after Joan made sure I was tortured to exhaustion. Just how many more times did I need to prove myself?

While the rest of the kids my age sat at desks, circling answers with pencils and stressing about college apps, I was in the woods learning how to make a fire from wet bark and identify which mush-rooms wouldn't kill me. My tests didn't have grades. They had consequences.

So why did I feel like I was failing?

I reached the end of the pool and touched the wall, flipped, and kicked off again. Down. Across the bottom. Up for air.

When my head broke the surface for the sixth time, a voice said,

"Ellie, we need to talk."

I squinted through the water. Red hair. Pale skin. Towel in one hand, no smile.

Adelina.

I didn't stop. I pushed off the wall and went under again. If I swam hard enough, maybe my thoughts would stop chasing me.

She was still there when I came up again. Standing at the edge like some clean-cut poster girl for *Covert Weekly*.

"Adelina," I said between breaths. "No disrespect, but I need to swim."

I dove under before she could argue, my legs slicing through the water, flippers propelling me to the opposite end. I surfaced, turned, and—

She was there.

Again. Holding the towel out like some kind of olive branch.

"I brought reinforcements," she said, voice steady.

I yanked my goggles off and wiped my face. The sun was blinding behind whoever stood beside her, making him glow like some kind of haloed saint. But when my vision adjusted, the man looked more mobster than holy.

He had a long jagged scar down one side of his face, a lean build wrapped in black, and that quiet, unnerving stillness that people who know too much tend to carry. The Priest? Maybe. Assassin? Possibly both.

He leaned down, and before I could react, his arms were under mine and he hauled me straight out of the pool. I flew a good three feet over the edge.

Midair, his suit jacket flared open—and I caught the glint of a holster and a weapon.

I landed hard on the concrete, blinking water from my eyes. "What sort of priest are you?"

Adelina chuckled and tossed me the towel again. "He gets that all the time."

I didn't move. I sat, wet and irritated, calculating how fast I could run if this turned sideways.

Adelina flopped into a chaise lounge and patted the one next to her. I didn't want to, but I sat anyway. The priest—Father Raphael—lowered himself into the one on my other side. His legs were so long they dangled like they belonged to a puppet that had outgrown the stage.

"Are you here to make sure I don't run?" I asked.

"Are you planning to run?" he asked without hesitation.

The way the shadow fell across his scar made him look like a man you didn't say no to.

Adelina smacked his knee. "Father Raphael. Stop."

He grinned. "Sorry. Too fun."

"We're here to encourage you," Adelina said, throwing him a warning look with her nose scrunched up.

"Right. Yes. Encouragement." He sat forward, arms on his knees. "You've got training. That's more than we had."

"What does that mean?" I asked, arms crossed tight.

Adelina met my gaze—not condescending, not sugarcoated, just steady. "Like I said in the briefing—I was fifteen when I volunteered to be bait. The trafficker had taken my best friend. I didn't have years of training or survival drills. Just one goal: get him to come after me so the team could take him down."

"Did it work?"

"Barely. It went sideways fast. But we caught him. And we stopped the chain before it reached more girls." She paused. "You have something I didn't, Ellie. A lifetime of training."

I felt something twist in my chest. Not emotion. Just recognition.

"I followed Ryszard," Father Raphael said suddenly. "The same trafficker. After my sister disappeared. I didn't have proof. Just a name and a gut feeling. I followed him to an abandoned building outside Warsaw. That's where I found the girls. Chained. Drugged."

He looked out over the pool like he was still there.

"I must have gasped. That's when he attacked me. Knife to the face. Knocked me out cold. When I woke up, they were gone. Including my sister."

Adelina's fingers gripped the edge of the lounge chair. Her voice was quiet when she said, "That one act started a task force. We've been taking down traffickers all over the world. Now we're here."

"With me," I said.

"With you," Father Raphael confirmed.

"You're ready, Ellie," Adelina added. "You're ready. It doesn't matter if you know how to use a phone or computer. What you need you already have."

"A team?" I asked as Annabelle, Cory, and Ezra joined us and plopped down on chaise lounges.

"I was going to say focus and quick wits."

I gave a quick wave to the teens. "Oh, hey!"

"Ellie, the schedule says you're supposed to be training us right now," Annabelle snorted.

"I'm game," Cory said.

While they were looking at each other and probably silently judging me, I let my towel drop and swung my legs to the side of the lounger and planted my feet.

Before Annabelle had time to react, I grabbed her and thrust her into the pool. Then I dived in after her.

Before her head surfaced, I pushed it back down and held it there long enough for her to thrash around, but not long enough to drown her. I let her up and she bobbed to the surface, gasped in a few deep breaths before yelling, "What the heck Ellie?"

"Rule number one. Stay calm. Don't struggle. Save your energy and breath so you can make a plan and escape."

Annabelle shook her fist at me, then turned to face Adelina and Father Raphael. "Hey aren't you a priest? You condone this sort of training?"

Father Raphael rose and said, "The Lord bless you and keep you," and made the sign of the cross. Then he turned to Adelina. "You're right. She is a lot like you."

"I feel confident that she is up to the task," Adelina said to Annabelle. "If you listen to her, maybe you will be too."

CHAPTER
THIRTEEN

ALIAS MEETS JACK RYAN: SECRETS, SCAVENGER HUNTS, AND SHADOW TECH

AS IF OUR team wasn't divided enough, the next two training sessions didn't go well. Annabelle was still miffed at me for holding her under water. When it was Ezra's turn to train us in the tech, I didn't understand any of the terms, and everyone lost patience with me. I hoped Cory would be on my side because he didn't get most of it either and kept saying, "Why does the muscle have to learn all this techy stuff?" But he wasn't.

Annabelle replied with, "If you graduated third grade, you'd be up to speed." Then she swung around and faced me with her hands on her hips. "Oh wait, you didn't go to school. Can you even read?"

After that comment, a voice came from the loud-speaker. "That's enough team."

A minute after the loudspeaker voice, Damica entered the lab. "Time for a group session."

"We're sticking to the schedule," I replied. Maybe if I stood up for the team, I'd get back on their good side.

Ezra looked at his watch. "Make it quick. I have a training with Maryanne in half an hour."

Cory leaned back in his chair, folded his hands behind his head, and said, "Fine by me doc. Profile away. I've got nothing to hide."

"You can say that again," Annabelle smacked him on the abs of his too-tight uniform.

Cory grinned and flexed.

Annabelle added, "All brawn and no brains."

He deflated like a poked balloon.

"Listen teens, if you can't get along, there is no way I'm approving you to go in the field."

"You mean it is up to you?" I asked, thinking back to what Adelina and Father Raphael had told me poolside. "I'm ready."

"You may be," Damica replied as she ran her slim fingers through her blonde curls. "But the team must function as one organism."

"And yes, Reggie has given me the power to excuse any one of you from the field."

"Oh," Annabelle said, and her face stayed frozen

with her lips in a small letter "o." Then she smiled. "What do you want us to do?"

We hadn't had our sit down profiles with Damica yet, but I had the feeling that she was evaluating our every move and maybe reading our thoughts and intentions. Like Shawn from *Psych*, nothing escaped her attention. I imagined her categorizing Annabelle as a chameleon as she was now sitting at attention and her "o" face had changed to a grin, looking like Damica was the most interesting person in the world. Cory, with his flexing, was smarter than he let on. Me: Awkward.

"Here's what we are going to do. I have set up a scavenger hunt. You won't need to leave Brightwood. Here's the first clue."

She held out the clue and Annabelle reached for it. Damica pulled it back and then put it in my hand. "Work together."

Damica left and I unfolded the first clue written on paper with the Brightwood emblem.

"Not made of stone, yet older than walls.

I've seen generations, heard secrets and calls.

My limbs stretch wide where the ravens convene—

Find what I cradle, beneath the green."

"I've got this one. Come on!" I stuffed the clue in my pocket and ran through the open doorway Damica had just left. I took the steps to the main floor two at a time. Once there, I exited the first door outside, the team following. I stopped for half a minute when I realized Ezra couldn't keep up.

"What is the hold up?" Cory pushed my back, sending me spiraling forward.

"Wait for Ezra," I commanded.

Ezra caught up and placed his hands on his knees. "I don't think I can keep up, guys. Go on ahead."

"Wait, Damica said we had to solve this together, not *be* together."

"What are you saying?" Annabelle asked. "Like he has to stay in the van?"

"You're a genius, Annabelle."

She smiled and puckered her lips. "Just doing my beautiful part."

I continued, "He can put those camera thingys on us and give us those ear things."

"I can see that you were kind of paying attention," Ezra replied when he caught his breath.

"Okay, we're losing time here." Cory held up his watch.

I'd forgotten Damica's last words: "You have one hour."

"Cory, can you carry Ezra back to the lab and grab what we need?"

Cory saluted and did a perfect squat. "Your trusty steed awaits."

Ezra hopped on his back and Cory took off.

"Great job using your strengths," Annabelle

yelled after him. I knew she probably meant it as a jab, but Cory took it as a compliment.

"Here to serve," he yelled back as the side door clicked closed after him, cutting off whatever else he said.

"Let's read the first clue again. I don't want to waste any time."

I pulled it from my pocket and read aloud as we walked in a tight circle, waiting for Cory and Ezra to return. "'Not made of stone, yet older than walls. I've seen generations, heard secrets and calls. My limbs stretch wide where the ravens convene—Find what I cradle, beneath the green.'"

Annabelle raised a brow. "Okay, that's definitely not a building."

"It's alive," I said, the wheels already turning. "It's not stone, not a statue—has to be a tree."

Before she could reply, the side door burst open and Cory strutted out, Ezra's gear slung over his shoulder.

"Your gadgets, m'lady," he said with an exaggerated bow, dropping a small case on the bench.

Ezra followed behind, slightly less breathless than before. "Cory's surprisingly fast for a walking protein shake."

"Flattering," Cory replied, handing out the comms. "Now, let's play spy."

Ezra helped Annabelle attach the mini cam to her

collar. "These should livestream to my tablet. I'll stay here and monitor."

I clipped mine on and popped the earpiece in. "Perfect. Damica said we had to *solve* it together, not *be* together. So you're still in the game."

"Remote brains are still brains," Ezra said with a shrug. "Just don't forget who's watching your six."

"Copy that, Control," I said, grinning as I turned toward the courtyard. "Alright—back to the clue. *'Seen generations, heard secrets'*—That's not just any tree. That's *the* oak."

Annabelle gasped. "The creepy one?"

Cory groaned. "The one that looks like it eats freshmen? Awesome."

"Exactly." I broke into a run. "It's older than anything here, and ravens nest in it—*'where the ravens convene.'* The last line—*'what I cradle, beneath the green'*—means we're looking under the leaves at the base. Come on!"

We raced across the lawn, the old tree looming ahead like it had been waiting centuries for us to show up.

We skidded to a stop beneath the gnarled branches of the ancient oak. It looked even bigger up close—like it could swallow secrets whole and never spit them out.

Cory bent over, hands on his knees. "Remind me why we're doing this voluntarily?"

"Because it's not just a game," I said, already scanning the mossy base. "Damica's testing us."

Annabelle crouched beside me, brushing away a pile of brittle leaves. "There's nothing obvious."

Ezra crackled into our ears. "Try the roots. Look for a split or hollow. Old trees sometimes have cavities where water drains."

"Smart," I said, nodding. "Ezra says check the root section."

We spread out, circling the base. I ran my hand along the bark until my fingers sank into something soft—a patch of damp earth tucked between two thick roots. I dropped to my knees and started digging with both hands.

"Found something," I called. "Help me clear it."

Cory joined me, scooping with his hands. I kept digging beside him, and then I saw his fingers stop. He had hit something hard.

"Got it!" He tugged, and a small metal box emerged from the dirt, crusted in mud and oak leaves. He handed it to me.

I popped the latch. Inside, wrapped in plastic, was a folded slip of paper and a strange copper key.

Annabelle leaned over my shoulder as I read aloud:

"Once I rang for meals and rule,
But now I sleep in shadows cool.
I faced the hall, I heard the bell—
But now I've lost my voice and dwell.

Behind the bricks, beneath the gaze,
I keep the key to Brightwood's maze."

We all exchanged a look.

"Creepy," Cory said.

Ezra's voice buzzed in again. "Sounds like an old dining hall or bell tower."

Annabelle checked her watch. "We've already used fifteen minutes."

That lit a fire under me. "Then we don't stand around. Let's move."

I tucked the second clue and the copper key into my jacket. "Let's find the next stop—before we fail the test and Damica doesn't approve us for the field."

We took off again, our feet pounding the path, leaves scattering in our wake.

We reached the chapel just as the sun crested over the trees, casting long, warm shadows across the overgrown lawn. My blazer stuck to my back, and Annabelle was already fanning herself with the edge of her clipboard.

"Next time," she huffed, "we vote on scavenger hunt season. Preferably not swimsuit weather."

The chapel doors creaked open with a push, revealing the cool, shadowy interior. Dust motes floated in thick bands of light, and the air smelled like old wood and candle wax. No one spoke as we stepped inside. Something about the place demanded quiet.

"Bell tower's this way," I said, leading them

toward the narrow staircase that curved upward along the stone wall.

Cory tugged at the collar of his uniform. "Pretty sure this wasn't built to code."

"Pretty sure you're not built for subtlety," Annabelle muttered, climbing behind him.

At the top, we ducked into the dusty tower. The bell hung overhead like a silent threat, thick with rust. Sunlight filtered through a broken panel near the roof, spotlighting a loose section of bricks at the base of one window.

"There," I said, already moving.

Annabelle spotted it too. "'*Behind the bricks, beneath the gaze…*' That's got to be it."

Cory crouched and pried the brick free with a grunt. Inside was a rolled scroll—neatly tied with twine and stamped with the Brightwood emblem in deep blue wax.

I cracked the seal and unrolled it carefully. Fancy, thick paper. Handwritten.

"The eyes that watch from painted walls,
See past the masks and whispered calls.
Where beauty waits in layered hue,
A hidden truth is framed for you."

"Painted walls," Annabelle echoed. "Portraits."

"Art hallway," I said. "Off the old staff wing. Remember? It's filled with portraits of Brightwood's founders."

Cory checked his watch. "We've got about thirty-five minutes left."

"And more than one clue to find," I said, tucking the scroll into the inside pocket of my blazer. "Let's go."

We bounded back down the stairs, shirts untucked and sweat clinging to our necks. As we burst into the sunlight, I couldn't shake the feeling that we were being watched.

We ran back to the main house and entered by the same door we'd exited earlier.

"Follow me," Annabelle yelled as she took the stairs two at a time.

When we arrived in the main hall, she paused suddenly. We stopped when Annabelle did, tumbling over like a set of dominos, Cory on top, knocking the breath out of us.

When he stood and straightened, he gave a quick "I'm sorry" before jerking me up to my feet. Annabelle lay on the floor, catching her breath for a few more seconds.

"Up one flight and to the left," she said, already half-standing. "The portraits are on the opposite end of the wing from our rooms."

Cory moved to pass her, but she caught him with an arm to the chest.

"This one's mine," she warned.

"I didn't realize we could claim clues," he grumbled.

Annabelle rose and, ignoring him, pointed to a portrait of a beautiful woman with raven colored hair and periwinkle eyes. "It has to be her. I mean I'd kill for eyes like that."

"You've been here before." It was a question, but I said it like a statement of fact.

"Yeah, I like to come look at the art," she said while she brushed a loose hair out of her face.

"What about '*The eyes that watch from painted walls, See past the masks and whispered calls*?" Cory asked.

"Uh, guys, ever get the feeling that someone is watching us?" Ezra said through our earpieces.

"Yes!" I shouted.

"So Cory is right. There is merit to that part of the clue and you passed it on the way up."

"What did we pass?"

"There are cameras in the walls and those portraits you are looking at have listening devices behind them."

"Score!" Cory pumped a fist in the air. "See it's not just *your* clue."

Annabelle punched him in the gut. "Was too."

"She's right. It is her clue," I intervened, trying to stave off an argument. We were losing time and the clock was ticking.

"I'll explain it later. Mind filling us in on the details when we solve the next clue, Ezra? During the running across the campus part. Get the clue, Annabelle."

Annabelle slid a hand behind the portrait and pulled out another clue.

"Score!" She imitated Cory's low voice and fist pump.

"Funny," Cory replied. "Read the clue."

"Electric whispers, long since ceased,
I fed on code, now I'm deceased.
My floppy heart no longer ticks,
But I once lived through circuits and clicks."

"If the last one was Annabelle's, this one is mine!" Ezra's voice crackled from the comms.

Cory grabbed the clue. "Where are we going, dude?"

"We, I mean…you…are going to the old computer lab in the forbidden sector."

"Sounds like we are in a Jack Ryan movie," Cory said as he ran down the stairs, leading the way.

"Who is Jack Ryan?" I asked as I ran two steps for every one of his.

Annabelle seemed content to take up the rear. Maybe because she'd gotten "her clue." "Tell us about the walls watching or whatever."

"So," Ezra began, "I've been looking into this place. It was converted around 1980 when the tech wasn't as sophisticated as it is now…"

"Then this might be Ellie's clue. Maybe it is in a room full of VCRs." She laughed at her joke.

I didn't want to argue. We were running out of

time. "Don't be ridiculous. The tree was mine." I linked arms with her and pulled her along.

"Turn right. Go down that hallway," Ezra continued. "Anyway, they put cameras in the walls as well as intercom systems they rigged to stay on the listen function."

"Creepy. I feel like Jack Ryan. We'll have to watch the series together." He paused at a crossroads. "Which way dude?"

"Go left and straight to the end of the hallway."

Cory took off and we followed.

This part of the building hadn't been used or cleaned in awhile. I ran through two cobwebs, sputtering out sticky web.

"Stay behind me if you don't want to eat spiders, Annabelle."

Cory reached the door first. "Man, there's a code. How much time do we have left?"

"Twenty-five minutes," Ezra replied.

"If this is your clue, I hope you figured out the code."

"Ezra, you getting this?" I whispered into the comm.

"Loud and clear," he replied, the faint clacking of his keyboard echoing in my ear. "Alright, break it down. 'Electric whispers'—something that used to run on power but doesn't anymore."

"Old tech," Annabelle said, leaning in. "Something obsolete."

"Exactly," Ezra said. "Next line—'*I fed on code, now I'm deceased.*' That means it ran on code, but it's no longer active. It's not a radio or a TV. It's something that relied on coded input."

"Computer?" Cory guessed, shifting his weight beside me.

"Bingo." Ezra's voice crackled with excitement. "And the next part—'*My floppy heart no longer ticks.*' That's the clue. Early computers used floppy disks for data storage. The floppy disk was literally the heart of the system."

I tightened my grip on the clue. "Okay, but that still doesn't give us a code."

"Actually, it does," Ezra cut in. "The original IBM PC—the one that popularized floppy disk drives—was released in 1981. It's considered the birth year of modern personal computing."

"1981," I repeated, glancing at the keypad next to the door. The metal buttons gleamed, taunting me. "You're sure?"

"As sure as I am that you're going to owe me pizza if I'm right," Ezra quipped. "Trust me—1981."

I reached for the keypad, my pulse thundering in my ears. Cory braced himself beside me, and Annabelle whispered a quick prayer.

I punched in the numbers.

1-9-8-1

The lock gave a sharp, metallic click.

Annabelle exhaled. "He did it."

The door groaned open an inch, revealing nothing but darkness.

"Nice work, Ezra," I whispered into the mic. "You just got us in."

It swung wider, and we stepped inside. My shoes scraped against the gritty floor, sending up little clouds of dust. The musty air hit us like an old, unwashed gym towel—one that had spent the last two decades steeping in stale cigarettes.

Cory pulled out his phone, swiping the screen until a bright beam cut through the darkness. Annabelle did the same, her phone's light dancing off the towers of ancient computer monitors and tangled cords.

I fumbled for my own phone, squinting at the screen. How did they make this look so easy? I tapped the screen a few times, swiped up, then down, then accidentally opened my weather app. Great, 82 and sunny. Not helpful.

Annabelle huffed, leaning over my shoulder. "You have to swipe down from the corner, Ellie. We've been over this."

"Right, right." I followed her instructions, and my phone finally spat out a weak beam of light, casting long shadows over the cracked linoleum and sagging office chairs. Note to self: practice basic phone functions before the next potentially dangerous mission.

"Seriously?" Annabelle muttered, her light bouncing off stacks of old computer towers and yellowed monitors. "We cracked all those clues for this? Not even a single balloon drop? No hidden treasure? Just... this?"

Cory waved his phone over a row of ancient desktops stacked like forgotten tombstones against the wall. "It's like the technology graveyard. Where dead modems go to rot."

I clicked off my light and dropped into a dusty, cigarette-stained armchair that groaned beneath my weight. I tried not to think about what kind of bugs might have made a home there. "Come on, guys. The scavenger hunt wasn't about a prize. It was a test—to see if we could work together. Think about it. We each solved one part."

Annabelle raised an eyebrow. "What are you talking about?"

"Ellie's right," Ezra's voice crackled through my earpiece. "The tree for Ellie. The belltower for Cory. The beautiful portrait for Annabelle. And the computer room for me. It was designed to see if we'd each lean into our strengths."

Cory flopped onto a nearby couch, sending a plume of dust into the air. "So we're the prize?"

"Exactly," I said, smirking. "Congratulations, Shadow Squad. We passed the test."

Annabelle rolled her eyes. "Great. Do I at least get a ribbon or something?"

I chuckled, leaning my head back against the musty upholstery, trying to catch my breath. For a moment, I let my eyes drift around the room, taking in the eerie, forgotten technology. Somewhere in the back of my mind, I made a note to buy a hazmat suit for our next adventure.

"Hey, Ellie," Ezra's voice crackled again, a sudden edge to it. "Pan left a bit. What's that on the shelf behind you?"

I sat up, turning my head slowly. I hadn't noticed it before—a bulky metal device, half-hidden behind a stack of old computer manuals. I reached for it, my fingers brushing against the cold metal. Dust clung to my hand as I pulled it into the light.

Scrawled in block letters across the side was a single word: **EREBUS.**

My pulse quickened. I turned it over, feeling the weight of it, the cool metal thrumming faintly in my grip. It was heavier than it looked. Old. Important. Like something that should come with a dramatic movie soundtrack.

"Bring that with you," Ezra said, his voice tight. "I want a closer look."

I barely had time to nod before a shrill alarm erupted from my wrist, the tinny, robotic beeping of the timer on my phone. I nearly dropped the device, my heart slamming into my throat. Annabelle let out a shriek, stumbling backward into Cory, who swore under his breath.

"Okay, okay, okay!" Cory panted, his hand over his chest. "We get it, time's up!"

Annabelle slapped at her wrist, trying to silence the noise. "Well, that's fitting. We just solved a massive puzzle for no prize, no confetti, and no balloons. I'm feeling really appreciated right now."

"Bring the device," Ezra repeated, his voice more serious now. "Whatever it is, it doesn't belong there."

I tightened my grip on the cold metal, the word EREBUS staring back at me like a challenge. I glanced at Cory, who was suddenly studying the ground a little too closely. My pulse spiked. Why did he look guilty? What did he know about this place that I didn't? I opened my mouth to ask, but heavy footsteps echoed from the hallway outside, the faint creak of the floorboards making my stomach drop.

Before I could react, the door creaked open, and Theo's silhouette filled the doorway, his eyes catching on the device in my hands.

"What did you find?" he asked, his tone too casual to be innocent.

I glanced down at the EREBUS device, my mind spinning. I had the sinking feeling we'd just stumbled onto something much bigger than a scavenger hunt.

PSYCH MEETS SPY KIDS: ORANGE PEELS AND DOUBLE AGENTS

WEEKS HAD GONE BY. Training, drills, fake missions, more drills. We'd passed the scavenger hunt and every shadowy test they'd slipped past us, like we were being prepped for a role no one would name.

And the real mission? Still nowhere. Like it had been quietly moved to a shelf marked *"someday"* and covered in dust along with the EREBUS, we'd stashed back in the computer lab.

The most dangerous op we'd performed had been riding the bus to get groceries at the Farmer's Market earlier today. Sure, we'd stuck fake listening devices in ten of the stalls. At one stall, the owner had thought Cory was stealing an orange.

"I know you rich prep school types," the hadn't-bathed-in-a-week earthy-looking woman with long ratty braids had said as she'd grabbed his arm. "You think you can get away with anything."

I had taken that opportunity to place a bug – which was really one of those small pads you put on furniture legs so it doesn't scratch the floor. Jim had suggested using those in case we got caught — we could say it was a game or challenge.

Cory had held both hands in the air. Annabelle had come to the rescue and smiled her best he-is-an-idiot smile. "Sorry, he really is a rich prep school type. Thinks he can get away with anything." She had punched him in the arm and added, "I'm a scholarship kid."

Earthy woman had handed Annabelle a bag of oranges. "Free of charge." She had turned and frowned at Cory. I had winked at Annabelle and we had been on our way.

"I think Cory should have to get that 'bug' and apologize," I suggested.

"If we didn't have to wear these uniforms, I'd have a better chance of blending in."

I straightened my blazer. "We do stand out, which makes it more of a challenge."

"That's Annabelle's strength," Ezra commented in our earpieces.

The scavenger hunt Damica sent us on weeks ago

had accomplished her agenda. We worked better as a team. Annabelle didn't fight me as much during exercises. But she still got in her jabs about my ignorance of the real world and technology.

For instance, when Agent Jim had handed us the furniture pads, she had blurted out, "These are about your speed…" She'd paused and added, "Wait… after seeing the dump you lived in you probably have no idea what these are."

"We do have target practice later on." I'd elbowed her in the side. "And that pink hair is a perfect target."

One thing I was learning about teens, even teen spies, was that verbal jabs and jokes were part of their coping mechanisms. We were all a lot more "Shawn and Gus" then I'd ever imagined. It was fun to play along with these verbal jousting sessions.

Annabelle hadn't answered my last jab because one, what could she say? She knew I could hit the ribbon out of her hair. And two, Jim had cleared his throat, and that was the signal to stop goofing around.

We finished our "bug planting" assignment and sat down on a bench to wait for the bus.

"Being a teen spy is nothing like the movies," Cory lamented. "They could at least give us a really cool car to drive."

"Well, not legally. Yet. But how about an Ethan

Hunt getaway? I'm very Mission: Reasonably Possible."

"Who is that?"

Annabelle opened the bag of oranges, pulled one out and began peeling it. "Your ignorance is showing."

"Be quiet, scholarship girl." I reached over and grabbed an orange.

"Sure, trailer park trash, help yourself." She flipped a piece of peel onto my plaid skirt.

"Girls, stop fighting," Ezra chided in the earpiece. "Do you have the device?"

We had our own sub-mission planned after the mission. I'd been sent to ask Reggie if we kids could go to a movie after our farmer's market fake bugging mission. I had been voted to be the one to go because I'd never been to a movie before.

The teen team had sent me specifically to Reggie because he seemed to like me more, at least that's what they had said. The truth is, if I'd gone to Agent Jim or anyone else, they would have reminded me of how important the mission was. Damica would profile me and figure out we were hiding something. We were. The EREBUS device.

When Theo had asked what we found at the end of our scavenger hunt in the room where computers go to die, I had hid it behind my back. Annabelle had jumped in front of me and talked nonstop for two minutes about the hunt, giving herself the credit for figuring every clue out.

We'd met later in my room so Ezra could examine the device.

"This is new tech guys."

We'd determined this device was not part of the scavenger hunt. But it may have something to do with The Alliance and the missing teens. Because we didn't trust meeting at Brightwood and discussing it with the adult team, we were going offsite. By offsite, I mean my trailer park, Shadow Pines.

The bus squeaked and snorted to a stop. I patted my backpack to make sure I still had the EREBUS and then stood. We filed on, blending in with all the riders. Looking like prep school kids on the way home from a field trip.

At the Brightwood corner stop, Ezra climbed on.

In fifteen minutes, we arrived at the edge of town. The last stop: Shadow Pines. We filed off, looking very different than when we got on. We had peeled off our blazers and skirts, revealing the ratty tees and shorts we wore underneath. Our uniforms got shoved into our backpacks as we pulled out summer flip-flops. Now we looked like we belonged here.

Satisfied we would blend in at the trailer park, I stepped off the bus first, looking for neighbors who would recognize me. No one. Good. I motioned to the rest of the team, who had disembarked to follow me.

I pulled a key out of my shorts pocket and clicked it into the lock of my door. I turned. It locked. What was going on here? Surely I locked it. I turned again and unlocked it, peering over my shoulder at my team.

"Back up. It was unlocked."

Annabelle and Ezra backed up. Cory crowded behind me instead. I didn't have a weapon and whoever opened the door may be inside. No time to go to the bunker and grab a crossbow. Not only that, but it was not exactly a weapon I could use in close quarters.

"Hand me an orange," I hissed at Annabelle.

"What are you going to do, squirt them?" Cory asked.

"No, I'm going to get some peel and shove it into their tear ducts."

"Dude you are—"

Before Cory finished, the door opened. I peered into the darkness while I grabbed a piece of orange peel. I stepped inside ready to fight or die. Probably die. What good would an orange peel be if they had a gun? I thought about sidestepping as soon as I entered. But that would mean Cory would die. So I plunged through, orange peel raised.

"I told you they would come here."

"I told you they were hiding something."

A chain rattled and light filled the living room.

"I told you she'd go it alone."

Kat, Damica, Adelina.

I stood in silent shock with the orange peel held over my head.

"What were you going to do with that?"

Cory stumbled and took in the three agents. "Oh, I guess the gig is up."

I lowered the orange peel and addressed them. "I was going to shove the bitter side of this in your tear ducts."

"Good plan," Kat said as she motioned to the door. "Tell the rest of them to come in."

I turned, pushed past Cory, and stepped in.

"Come in guys. It's safe." I said that, but I wasn't sure.

Why and how had they found us? And where were Agents Jim and Nathaniel?

"Jim and Nathaniel thought you'd actually go to the movies," Kat said as she slapped her knee. She laughed and added, "We won the bet."

The three women agents high-fived each other, ignoring us as we sunk into chairs Cory dragged from the dinette.

Damica turned after the high-five session and pushed a blonde curl out of her eye. "What did you find in the computer room?"

"How can we be sure we can trust you?" I shot back.

"Kat and Adelina, meet younger you."

Annabelle crossed her arms and leaned back in a

defiant pose. "Enough with the psychoanalyzing mumbo jumbo and give us a reason to trust you."

"Yes, you say we're agents, but you treat us like we're…" Cory paused as he searched for a word. "Stupid."

"Yeah. You sent us to stick furniture stickers in stalls at the Farmers Market," I added and crossed my arms.

"That was Jim's idea," Kat said and stood. "We know what it's like not to be trusted as an agent." She did a sweep of her arm to include Adelina and Damica.

"Yeah," Damica chimed in. "People think I'm a teenager and therefore…what's the word you just used Cory?"

"Stupid," we four teens said in unison.

Adelina ran her fingers through her fiery red hair. "And because I was fifteen when I went undercover for the first time, the agents in charge didn't share all the information with me, so I messed up and almost got killed."

"So why are you doing it to us?" I responded. "Yes, we found something, but you knew it was there and you didn't tell us."

"We didn't know it was there." Kat rocked back and forth. "We thought it might be at Brightwood."

She stopped and tapped her head. Then, with a hand on her hip, she pointed at each of us.

"Each one of you has something to hide. Come now, am I right?"[1]

We'd just been talking about how no one had clued them in when they were new agents, how unfair it had been. Then somehow the conversation pivoted, like it always does with adults, to *us*—how we weren't sharing enough, how we were keeping secrets.

Wasn't that the point of spy training? That everyone lies?

"Is this an interrogation?" I stood and faced her, nose to… well, her chin, because she's tall like a birch tree.

"Was that a quote from *The Murder of Roger Ackroyd?*" Annabelle asked.

No one answered her. Everyone was silent.

They knew we'd found *something*. And now we knew they'd been looking for *something*. We didn't say the name stamped across the side of that metal block in the computer graveyard. We didn't have to. Their faces said enough.

Cory stepped in between Kat and me, shoving me back into my seat. "If we found what you think we found, why do you want it?"

Annabelle shot up out of her seat. "This mission wasn't about saving the teens at all, was it?"

"It was about whatever you are looking for." I stood and swung my backpack onto my shoulder. "And we were sent on a scavenger hunt to find it."

"Let's go, guys," Annabelle said, reading my mind. "We have a movie to watch."

I didn't wait for an answer from the agents. I knew the answer. We were being used and this little group session of I-know-how-you-feel and we-were-you was all about getting the device. Now to figure out what it was and why it was more important than the life of thirty teens. Thirty-four if you counted us.

PSYCH VS. THE PARENTING FILES: SECRETS, SELFIES, AND SUSPICION

OUR DRAMATIC EXIT turned out to be anticlimactic. In the *Psych* episodes, when Shawn and Gus left the cop station in a flurry of smart remarks and "psychic readings," they either went to get something to eat or they went home. Damica, Kat, and Adelina were in my home. No one else in the group had a home other than Brightwood. We had no money. Just a bag of oranges.

"I'm not ready to go back to Brightwood yet and walk the hall of shame," Annabelle announced, giving voice to my musings.

Ezra, still scrolling through his tablet beside us, broke the silence. "Theo just messaged. He wants the device handed over the second we get back."

I instinctively patted my backpack, as if it could tell me what to do.

"We need to regroup," I said, right as the bus pulled up with a brake screech loud enough to swallow the word "group" whole.

We filed on and plopped down on the long row in the back of the bus.

"You know…" I glanced out the window behind me. "It won't be hard for them to follow us and take the device."

"That's true," Cory turned and followed my gaze. The agents weren't at the bus stop. Surely they were grabbing a vehicle to follow us. "And they probably have a really cool car."

I reached up and pulled the bus line, signaling the bus driver to stop and let us off.

The bus driver turned and chuckled. "Kid, we haven't pulled out yet."

"Oh, right," I said as I stood and grabbed my backpack. "Sorry."

I turned to the others—and yeah, Ezra was right there, so no need for secret agent radio drama. "We've got to go off-grid. Like now-now."

We clambered off the bus in a mess of limbs and half-formed plans, bumping into each other like a spy team built entirely from outtakes.

Ezra was already digging through his backpack, pulling out a black pouch. "Phones off. Into this. No signals. No screw-ups."

Cory perked up. "Wait—do we get to smash them now? I've dreamed of this moment."

"No," Ezra said flatly. "This equipment costs more than my last hospital stay. Just power them down and stick them in the pouch."

We huddled behind the thin birch trees lining the edge of Shadow Pines while everyone made The Great Sacrifice—dropping our phones into the Faraday pouch like we were sealing a time capsule we hoped no one would ever find.

I led us around the perimeter—past flickering porch lights, a broken trampoline, and at least one cat that stared at me like it knew I was lying about everything. The gravel crunched beneath our feet as we reached the hidden entrance to the underground bunker.

"We'll wait in here until we figure out what comes next," I said, ducking through the low concrete opening.

"Ew, we have to go *back* in there?" Annabelle snapped, gripping her pink hair like it was in danger.

"Just until we're clear," I said. "Besides, if we're going off-grid, we'll need more than oranges and sarcasm. And this place? Stockpile central."

I motioned to Cory and he helped me pull the moss off the hidden door.

I pulled it open and light beamed out like a giant flashlight.

"Come on down," Kat called.

"Great plan," Annabelle hissed.

My first thought was to run. But they would follow. I'd read up on Adelina and how she'd tracked a group of mountain men traffickers up and down a mountain. She'd find us no matter where we hid in the woods. My plan deflated like a hot air balloon coming back to the earth with a thud.

I half expected them to have weapons pointed at us when we descended into the bunker. They didn't. All three of them sat comfortably on camping chairs.

"Joan told us you'd probably come here," Kat explained.

"I would have figured it out," Damica said, defending herself.

"We literally saw them getting off the bus," Adelina answered, followed by a chuckle. "You can't count that as profiling."

Kat ignored them and stuck out a hand. "I think we got off on the wrong foot back there."

"You mean the wrong foot where you waited at my house to get the EREBUS?"

Kat blinked. "The—what? That's not..." She glanced at Adelina and Damica, clearly thrown.

I turned to Damica and wagged my pointer finger at her. "Or the fact that you set up the whole scavenger hunt so we would find it."

Damica's brows shot up. "Wait—what are you talking about? What even is the EREBUS?"

"Yeah," I snapped. "Either we're agents working

with you or we're just disposable like the other teens."

"What do you mean?" Adelina rose to her feet, eyes wide. "That's not how we work. We don't use agents like that."

"Then who fed the thirty teens to The Alliance?" I asked.

I examined their faces. Shock. Surprise. No guilt. Cory swallowed hard as if he had a marshmallow stuck in his throat. Was that guilt or fear?

Annabelle stepped between me and the adult agents. "We're not giving it to you."

"What does it do?" Cory asked.

"The what now?" Adelina asked, glancing at Damica like she was hoping one of them had even heard the word before. "We didn't assign anything called EREBUS. What are you talking about?"

Kat shook her head. "Is this something you found on the scavenger hunt? Because that wasn't part of the original mission. Not from us."

"Let's all just take a step back and take a deep breath," Kat added, trying to regain control.

"We are all on the same team," Damica said, her voice calm and therapist-smooth, like we were just in need of a group hug and a grounding exercise.

"No. No. No," I answered as I attempted to pace. With the confined space, it turned into a cha cha.

"People who are on the same team tell each other what's really going on."

"Yeah, what's really going on?" Annabelle said.

"Sit down and we'll tell you everything we know."

"What do you mean everything you know?" I remained standing.

"I don't think Theo and Vivian are being completely honest with us. Let's start there…" Kat began.

"That's why we wanted to talk to you off-site," Damica continued and motioned for us to take seats on the camping chairs they'd set up.

I sat on the edge of an orange one, hands on my thighs, ready to flee if I needed to.

"Here's what we know," Kat continued. "We think the thirty teens were taken for The Alliance. They plan to train them, brainwash them and use them for their purposes."

"You've been to the underground training center," Cory stated.

"Yes, didn't you read the file or watch the news? She was supposed to assassinate the President of the United States."

Kat stood and folded her arms across her chest. "Yes, I was. America's Future lured in foster teens who were aging out of the system with the promise of an education and jobs."

"But those jobs were usually illegal and after a

recruit completed the job, America's Future let them take the rap, or killed them in some unfortunate accident," Adelina interjected. "Which is why I was astounded that you thought we would do that to you."

"Using foster kids as if they are disposable is what we are fighting against."

"So why off-book? Shouldn't we just rescue the teens?" I asked.

Kat looked thrown. "Rescue them from what? What is the EREBUS?" Her words stumbled over each other, like she was trying to backtrack and calculate at the same time. "Are you saying The Alliance is after this thing? That they're... willing to trade for it?"

Ezra jumped in before anyone could answer. "We found it during the scavenger hunt," he said carefully. "I scanned it. It's not normal tech."

Adelina's brow furrowed. "Then what is it?"

Ezra's voice dropped. "It connects. Passively. Phones, mostly. But it's not just syncing—it's rewriting. Quietly."

Kat went still.

"Theo showed up at the end of the hunt," I added. "He didn't act surprised we found something —he just wanted to know exactly what."

Annabelle crossed her arms. "We didn't tell him. We stashed it. Back in the computer room where old tech goes to die."

Cory, still seated, leaned in. "It's still there?"

Ezra didn't answer. None of us did.

Kat stood abruptly. "Ellie, we need to go."

"What?"

"The other reason we wanted to meet outside of Brightwood is I need you on a sub-mission."

"What's the mission?"

"We need to go to the prison and visit your mother and Lilith."

"The woman who trafficked you and shot Senator Helms?"

"Yes," Kat said as she brushed some dirt off her trousers. "Are you in?"

An op that didn't require me to hide furniture protectors at the farmers market or ride the bus to go shopping? Heck yeah, I was in. Then I thought about everything we'd just said about being a team. I gave Annabelle a quick glance.

"Yes, go see your mother," she said. "It's not like it is a real mission, right?"

"Nope. Just information gathering," Kat assured her.

"Ezra can tell us about the device," Cory said. "We'll fill you in later. Go see your mom."

Ezra nodded his agreement, and Kat and I climbed out of the bunker, brushing the dust from our clothing. She glanced at my backpack. "Do you have your uniform in there?"

"I do," I replied, adjusting the straps.

"You can change in the car." She stopped short and giggled, her eyes sparkling with a mix of relief and triumph.

"What's so funny?" I asked, glancing over my shoulder like maybe I'd missed some hidden camera.

"I didn't tell Jim we won the bet."

"Oh." I smirked. "Nice."

"Can you do a selfie with me so I can send it to him?"

I hesitated, then forced myself to nod. I was glad I at least knew what a selfie was from watching *Psych*. A little part of me felt a strange rush of connection, like maybe we were bonding over our quirks. I mean, I wouldn't have made it through the last few weeks without Kat's endless stream of murder mystery quotes. We were an odd pair, sure, but we got each other in a way that felt like… well, something more than just teammates.

I stepped beside her and smiled, trying not to look as awkward as I felt. She held her phone up at arm's length, angling it just right. "What should I say?"

"What?"

"I mean, what's a good slam? Like, 'You lost, loser?'"

I ran my hands through my hair, my mind flicking through my *Psych* database like I was scrolling through a playlist. All I could think of were Shawn's ridiculous one-liners.

"Okay, how about, 'Next time, trust the instincts, not the ticket stubs. We just solved this mystery with a side of nachos.'"

Kat burst out laughing, her finger hitting the shutter button mid-snort. "Perfect. He's going to hate that."

For a moment, the tensions and half-formed suspicions I'd felt earlier seemed to dissolve into humidity. All the false starts and side glances, the unspoken doubts about whether I could trust anyone here, felt like they'd been scrubbed away in this one small, ridiculous moment. Maybe, just maybe, we weren't all playing our own secret games. Maybe some of us really were on the same team.

Kat led me to a forest green Toyota Highlander, not the dark SUV I expected an FBI agent to drive.

I opened the passenger door and glanced to the middle captain seats that housed two car seats.

"You have kids?" I asked, trying to hide the surprise in my voice. I wasn't doing a great job at following my mom's number one rule. Blend in. Here I was going to visit her with one of the top agents in the world. One who didn't hide the fact that she had kids. She drove around with car seats and toys. And her vehicle of choice shouted "family."

In that moment, I realized how angry I was with my mother for hiding me. Making me live off the grid for most of my life. She trained me to be a spy without telling me who she was. Who *I* was.

As I slid into the seat, Kat said, "Yes, I have four kids all through adoption. Two in college and two in car seats." She adjusted her rearview mirror and smiled at the seats as if they had children in them. "Three girls – Helena and Jordan, both in college. Lousia and Edmund use the car seats."

Car seats? Really? Here I was, about to visit my super-spy mom with one of the world's top agents, and she rolls up in a Toyota Highlander that screams "soccer mom." I bet there's a baby wipe shortage wherever she goes.

And she has four kids? I glanced back at the car seats. *Two in college and two in diapers? That's not a family, that's a small battalion. I don't even know what it's like to have one sibling, let alone three. Does she take them to the park and teach them evasive maneuvers on the playground?*

"I read in your file about Lilith…" I paused, not knowing what to say next.

"That's a conversation shift. From kids to Lilith." She uncapped a thermos and poured herself a cup of coffee into a tiny mug that read **Deja Brew**. "Want some espresso?"

"No. Thanks." I fumbled with my buckle.

Kat reached over and snapped my seatbelt into place like a mom on autopilot. *Smooth, Ellie. You can rappel down a five-story building, but car safety is where you choke.* Mom would've told me to figure it out myself, probably while dropping me in the middle of a frozen lake for "training."

"I don't ride in cars much," I explained.

She ignored the comment. "I probably have some Reese's Big Cups in a cooler back there. One of our consultants, Bennie, can't live without them."

I'd read about him. Bennie—autistic, brilliant, and basically a human recorder. He remembered everything from license plates to the exact number of Reese's Big Cups Kat owed him.

I'd follow that thread later. Lilith was the priority.

I turned and found the cooler on the floor. Yep. Lots of Reese's Big Cups. I'd never had one. I wasn't going to tell her that. Mom and Joan kept me on a strict diet of no junk. Sure Joan slipped me the occasional energy drink, but thinking back on it, it was most likely so I could keep training.

The connection we had a moment ago had dissolved into a you-don't-belong mist. I grabbed one and pulled back the orange wrapper and stuck the whole thing in my mouth and savored the most chocolatey peanut butter goodness on the planet.

"Processed food is the enemy, Ellie. It'll dull your senses, slow your reflexes." Well, sorry, Mom, but if loving this chocolate-covered sugar bomb is wrong, I don't want to be right.

"That's exactly how Bennie eats them. I think you two would get along."

She downed her espresso, set the cup down, and punched the start button. "You were asking about Lilith?"

A stream of gooey goodness dribbled down my chin. Kat put the Highlander in reverse, glanced at me, saw my distress, and pointed to the glove box. "There are wipes in there."

I opened the glove box and pulled a crinkly pack of wipes out. After wiping my mouth and chin, I continued. "I mean Lilith was like a mom to you, right?"

We pulled onto the highway and she glanced at the screen. "Before I answer, could you plug an address in the GPS for me?"

She handed me the phone she'd grabbed from a cubby under the screen and recited an address for the Correctional Facility. "Hit the little square that looks like a map."

I fumbled with the phone, feeling like I was defusing a bomb. Okay, not really, but it felt high stakes. The most advanced tech I'd handled was a two-way radio Mom swore had saved her life more times than I could count. I bet Kat's kids could work this thing in their sleep.

"Oh," I said, feeling dumber than ….I don't know, a squirrel trying to hotwire a spaceship. I plugged the address in and pushed go.

A British woman's voice spoke from the screen. "Stay on highway 28 for ten miles, then turn left on …"

"Yes, Lilith was the counselor in Green Pines, the group home I was in. She took me under her wing."

She sighed. "Then she trafficked me. That's the short version."

I shifted in my seat, not sure if I should continue. I swallowed. "Your file said she tried to drown you in Spruce Lake in the dead of winter."

She gripped the steering wheel tightly, her knuckles whitening. "Yes. That's true. But not long after that, she repented of her actions and became a Christian."

"And then shot Senator Helms the next day?"

"Yes, that's true."

"So why are we going to see her?"

"Now you sound like Jim." She flushed red. "He says not to trust her. But I do every time."

"So we go and talk to her and not trust her."

"Do you trust your mom?"

"Not anymore." Before I could explain, a car zipped up behind us, swerved into the driver's side and ran us off the road. Kat jerked to avoid a tree as I braced myself for impact.

Of course, we couldn't just have a normal road trip, chatting about past trauma and questionable life choices. No, we had to add "run off the road by armed thugs" to the itinerary. Thanks, Mom, for making me paranoid enough to brace for impact before the crash.

She missed the tree only to hit another one with a sickening crunch. I flew forward, the seat belt cinched and a huge white bag opened and softened my landing. I was covered in powder released by the bag. It stung my face and neck. I clicked open the seatbelt and tumbled out. I stumbled to Kat's side. There was no one there.

"Ellie," a bush hissed. "Come on, let's go."

I glanced in the direction the car had come from and understood why Kat was hiding. Two black-suited bulky men jogged through the muddy ruts the Highlander had just made. I'd give anything for my crossbow right now.

We were unarmed, exposed and totally on our own. I slipped behind the bush with Kat. She motioned for me to hit the ground. I shook my head and grabbed her wrist and pointed to the woods. I appreciated that she was trying to protect me. But hiding in a bush was the worst idea. They always find you. You had to go somewhere they wouldn't expect.

We'd loop around the woods and go back to the road. Sure, staying in the woods would have been my first choice if I had my weapons. But I had nothing. So Plan B: hope no one stayed at the SUV that ran us off the road.

Kat and I ran a quick half-circle and ended up a few hundred feet from the SUV.

"You know how to drive that?" I pointed from my place behind an ancient oak tree.

"Yep. If they left the keys."

"Looks like they left one man to guard the vehicle," I whispered. "I'll handle him and you check for keys."

"Handle him? With what?"

I grinned. "Sweep the leg."

With that, I jogged to the back of the SUV and shimmied under it. *Okay, Ellie, think. You've trained for this. Sure, you trained with wooden dummies and holographic projections, not beefy guys with a wrestling fetish, but still.* What would Shawn do? Probably make a ridiculous joke and then pull off a miracle. Or at least insult the guy's shoes before getting tossed in a trunk.

Sweeping the leg from this vantage point was going to be difficult. I rolled out and tapped him on the bulging calf. He turned to see who was behind him. I leaped to my feet and hoped I had the time and strength to follow through with my plan.

"There you are." He reached for the backpack I'd slung over my shoulder. "Is this it?"

I swung my leg with all my strength and it landed on what felt like steel. My bones reverberated inside my calf. He chuckled, his face scrunched up as he studied the inside of my backpack.

"It's not here," he said.

I tried another tactic: I ran. It failed. He caught me by my blazer and flung me over his shoulder. Once I was deposited in the back of the SUV and secured, he unclipped a walkie-talkie from his belt and said,

"I've got the kid. She doesn't have the device." He walked away from the SUV as he talked.

The SUV shifted into gear and, with a jolt, bumped onto the highway. It picked up speed and I watched the man drop the walkie-talkie and chase the SUV.

Kat sat up and pressed the accelerator, evidenced by the man growing smaller in the distance.

"That was close," she said.

I sighed and leaned back against the backseat.

After a minute of silence, I asked, "Where are we going?"

"To the prison. To talk to Lilith and your mom."

"Won't *they* find us?"

"You think they'll follow us inside a prison?"

"Good point."

"More importantly we need to find out what the EREBUS is and why they want it."

I sat bolt upright. "You don't know?"

"Of course not. I didn't even know it existed until Theo told us."

"You didn't use us to find it?"

"Of course not. We came to rescue the thirty teen agents from The Alliance."

PRISON BREAK PSYCHOLOGY: TRUST, TRAUMA, AND TOYOTA SURVEILLANCE

ONCE AT THE PRISON, we moved through security quickly before going our separate ways—me to talk to my mom and Kat to talk to Lilith, the counselor from Green Pines who'd trafficked her. Oh, and shot Senator Helms.

Sure, I was mad at my mom for lying to me pretty much my whole life, but my anger would have to take a back seat to the other problems. Like getting her out of jail, freeing the thirty teens, and finding out what the EREBUS was and why it was hidden at Brightwood Academy. So many unanswered questions.

I wondered if Agent Jim knew his wife was at the

prison to talk to Lilith, and if we could trust her. Jim had said not to.

With all the questions swirling about in my mind, the first thing I said to my mother was, "Can we trust Lilith?"

"Well, hello to you too," she answered, followed by, "What are you doing here?"

"Hello, Mother. I found out you've been training me my whole life to be a spy. That's what I'm doing here," I said loudly and pounded my fist on the plastic table. The guard flinched and leaned forward as if she were prepared for action.

"Calm down, Ellie, and watch what you say."

"I'm not playing by your rules anymore. I've blended in so much I don't exist anymore. Living off the grid my whole life and for what? To be a teen spy."

She leaned forward and grasped my hand. "That's not what I intended for you. I was trying to keep you safe."

"Well, I'm not safe. On the way here, Agent Kat and I were…" I paused and studied my mom's face. I didn't want to get her killed while she was in prison, so maybe talking about the spy life wasn't a good idea. I shifted in my seat. "I meant to say, we got a flat tire."

"That's too bad." She nodded at the guard, who turned and opened the door. It shut with a loud thud, leaving us completely alone.

"I meant to tell you all about the spy life. But now's not the time."

"When is the time?"

"We only have a few minutes. I bribed the guard." She grabbed both my hands and pulled me closer. "I didn't murder anyone. I'm here on a mission. To gather intel about…"

"The Alliance," I whispered.

"Yes." She let go of my hands and sat back in her seat.

"From Lilith," I continued.

"I guess you're up to speed."

"Why did Joan pretend to be executed?"

"What?"

"She staged it. Then had her own men grab me—hood over my head, dragged into a van, shoved into some underground cell like I was the enemy. They asked about Brightwood—why I was there, what I did—again and again, like they were testing me."

My throat tightened. I hadn't realized how much that still lived under my skin.

"They never used the word 'spy,' but they didn't have to. That whole setup was designed to break me down. To see if I'd admit something. Slip up. Give you away."

"I never told Joan to do that." Her voice was firm, but something flickered behind her eyes. "I told her to protect you. That was it."

"Well, Mom, Brightwood needs protecting."

"From whom?"

"We found something there. The EREBUS."

As soon as the word left my mouth, I wished I could reel it back in. I switched gears fast. "Agent Kat and I were run off the road. We escaped."

"What is it?" she asked, zeroing in, completely ignoring the part where I almost died.

"I don't —" Before I could say the word "know," the guard was back. Mom and I spent our last few minutes chatting about nothing except the weather, and she asked me if I'd made any new friends. If I was liking the group home.

I met Kat outside the prison. She was waiting on the sidewalk.

I took a step toward where the SUV we'd arrived in *should* be. It wasn't there. Someone had come and removed it, which meant someone could be waiting in the parking lot for us. I scanned the area, looking for anyone suspicious. A bright blue Toyota RAV4 honked and pulled up. The tinted window rolled down and Maryanne stuck her head out.

"Need a ride?"

"How did you…?" I asked. My words hung in the air, unanswered, as I opened a back passenger door and climbed in.

I didn't need an answer, really. By now, I should've guessed there was some kind of tech tracking us. I never understood that stuff. Algorithms, pings, encrypted signals—it all felt like magic disguised as science.

Give me a deer trail any day.

I liked tracking in the woods. No screens. No code. Just instinct and observation. Smashed-down grass, broken branches, fresh scat, claw marks on bark. The woods made sense. Patterns made sense.

People didn't. And tech? Even worse.

Which got me thinking. If Kat said Lilith's pattern was to lie and then try to kill her, what if that was exactly what she was trying to do again? It was the pattern. The same comforting allure of a well-worn deer trail—pressed-down grass, broken twigs, and freshly turned earth leading you deeper into the trees. You follow, thinking you've got the upper hand, and then—boom, you're the one bleeding out in the snow.

Maryanne and Kat chattered in the front seat about our encounter on the highway.

"I knew you got away because, why would they take you to the prison?" Maryanne smacked the steering wheel as if she'd just told a joke and followed it with a high-pitched giggle.

I patted Kat's headrest. "Did you learn anything from Lilith?"

"She doesn't know what the EREBUS is either."

Maryanne hit the brake so hard my nose smashed into the headrest. When the car stopped, a trickle of blood dripped down onto my upper lip and pooled there. I wiped it with my sleeve.

"You told Lilith we had the EREBUS?" Maryanne and I said in stereo.

"Yes, she promised to help us." Kat pushed a strand of hair behind her ear.

"When have we heard that before?" Maryanne asked as she tapped the gas, putting us back in slow motion. I had the feeling this conversation was a rerun.

"I'll tell you. When she said her son Devon wasn't a trafficker, then shot Bennie. When the FBI released her from jail to help us take down America's Future…" As Maryanne talked, she pressed on the gas so the speed of the car matched her accelerating lecture. "Then she pushed you onto the ice on Spruce Lake…"

"Slow down, Maryanne, or you're going to kill us!" Kat braced herself by grabbing the door handle.

I did the same. I'd only been in a car a handful of times—but considering how those rides had gone, running through the woods might've been the safer bet. I didn't think I liked cars. I felt safer on a bus. On a bus, I wasn't being chased, or thrown in the back for a spin around the block before being tortured, or speeding down the highway by an angry woman.

I leaned forward again, my eyes on the back of Kat's head. "Lilith promised to help us? That's like a hunter whispering to a deer 'Hey, follow me. It's totally safe over here.'"

"But she is a Christian now," Kat pleaded.

"She is still a human who may be trapped in The Alliance's web." Maryanne evened out to what felt like a more reasonable speed. "And didn't she tell you she got sucked into America's Future, even though she hated what she was doing?"

"I'm calling Jim," Kat said and pushed a button on the screen of the RAV4.

"Jim, it's me, Kat. I messed up."

After Kat told Jim she'd asked Lilith about the EREBUS—and laid out what Ezra suspected it could do—there were a lot of words. Defensive, skeptical, layered with things unsaid.

Then silence. The kind that stretches taut like a wire, ready to snap.

In the middle of it, the Toyota RAV4 rolled up to the back entrance of Brightwood.

Kat clicked the screen and ended the call without another word.

I hopped out, already looking for the closest side door. I wanted to be inside, away from the road, away from the danger, away from the uncomfortable human conversations I wasn't wired for. Give me a dark hallway or a dense forest over this any day. I might not be able to read people, but I could read shadows and tree branches like a second language.

As I walked toward the door, I thought about that

episode of *Psych* where Shawn and Gus got kidnapped. Shawn was still cracking jokes while tied up in the back of a moving vehicle, like getting kidnapped was just another Tuesday. I wasn't wired like that. I'd calculate the length of the rope, the tensile strength of the knots, and how many seconds I'd have to break free before they dumped me in the nearest river.

People like Shawn could crack a joke under pressure. I just cracked.

———

Once in my room, I went to the bathroom and turned on the faucet in the tub. While waiting for it to warm up, I grabbed a clean tee and sweats from the closet. I tossed them onto the closed toilet seat. With the tub plugged, I let it fill halfway before adding bubbles. I swished my hand in the water, and the bubbles multiplied, climbing higher like fresh snow on a quiet winter morning.

I peeled off my uniform and let it fall to the floor, then tested the water with a toe before climbing in. The bubbles covered my body like a comfy flannel shirt, and the tension in my shoulders started to melt away. I closed my eyes and hummed the *Psych* theme song, letting the familiar notes push the chaos of the past few hours to the back of my mind.

As soon as I got out, I'd watch my favorite

episode—*The Spelling Bee*. I tried to focus on it, on Shawn standing in the booth, tossing out words like "onion" and "banana" just to mess with the judges, his grin daring someone to call his bluff. No plan, no strategy, just instinct and confidence. It always worked for him.

I sank a little deeper into the water, letting the warmth soak into my bones. Maybe that's why I liked Shawn so much. He made chaos look easy. He didn't overthink every step. He just went for it, trusted his gut, and somehow landed on his feet every time. I could respect that.

The adults here? They were a different story. All that training, all those tactical drills, and now they were fumbling around like rookies on their first field mission. They had made a plan—to plant me in The Alliance, let me sniff out the truth about the missing teens from the inside. But now they were second-guessing themselves, reacting to every bump in the road like nervous deer spooked by a snapping twig.

I'd seen it before. Not in real life—on *Psych*, Season 4, Episode 14: "Think Tank." In the episode, they brought in a room full of so-called experts to protect a billionaire, and it spiraled fast. Everyone started yelling out worst-case scenarios—snipers in the vents, poisoning the water, disabling the security grid—until nothing made sense anymore. The feed cut out, the client bailed, and later Shawn realized the guy running the session was using their scattered ideas to plan the real attack. At the speech, Shawn had to shove the billionaire out of the way because the sniper *actually* came from one of their ridiculous pitches.

That's what this felt like. A plan ripped up and replaced with random panic. No strategy. Just noise.

"I think we need to do something," Annabelle's voice said from behind me. I swiveled my bubble-covered neck to face her.

"Yeah, the adults aren't doing anything except training us," Ezra added.

"If you call planting stickers at the farmer's market training," Cory said as he sat on the tile floor next to my uniform.

"Guys, in the bath, here," I said, sinking down as far as I could in the bubbles.

"Not like we can see anything," Annabelle retorted. "That's some bubble bath. What are you, five?"

"Not that I didn't try to see something," Cory said with a smirk.

"I'm being a gentleman," Ezra reported.

Cory uncrossed his legs and jumped to a squat before standing and addressing Ezra. "No, you're not, dude. You only have eyes for Maryanne. A married woman."

Before I thought about what I was doing, I stood and pointed to the door. "Okay, everyone out."

Annabelle threw me a towel, which I wrapped around my sudsy body before Cory turned around.

"We will continue this conversation when I'm dressed."

"Can I..." I pushed Cory out the door and slammed it behind him before he could finish the sentence.

I shoved my leg into my sweatpants.

Fully dressed, I joined the teens in my bedroom.

"I agree with you, Annabelle. We need to do something."

"I already have," Ezra said. He clicked a few keys on his computer.

We huddled around Ezra's laptop, the tiny bug broadcasting the adults' meeting like a low-budget spy thriller. The screen glowed in the dim light of my room, the tiny waveforms on the audio file jumping with every sharp word from Jim.

Ezra nudged the angle slightly. "Mini cam in the bookshelf. Got audio too."

"Kat, you crossed the line. You gave Lilith critical intel, and now she knows about the EREBUS. What were you thinking?"

Kat's voice crackled back, a little shaky but defiant. "I was trying to find out what she knew. We need to figure out what we're up against."

Jim's frustration practically vibrated through the speakers. "You put us all at risk. You put *yourself* at risk."

Adelina's voice cut in, sharp and clear. "Then why haven't you sent Ellie in yet? She's ready."

I leaned in closer, my heart pounding. Finally, someone who saw what I could do.

Father Raphael's deep, reassuring voice followed. "I agree. She's had the best training, and she's the only one young enough to blend in with those kids."

Damica's scoff came through, sharp and dismissive. "She's also lived off the grid too long. She knows nothing about the real world. She doesn't know how to blend in with city kids or navigate their social structures."

I felt my jaw tighten. I'd lived off the grid, sure, but that didn't make me clueless. I could blend in when I needed to. I'd survived in places where people like Damica would stick out like a neon sign.

Joan jumped in, her voice tinged with exasperation. "That's not fair, Damica. She's had the best training of anyone here. She can handle it."

Ezra shot me a quick look, his eyebrows raised. I just shrugged, trying not to let the sting of Damica's comment show on my face.

Then Lassiter's gravelly voice cut through the static. "If we're moving in, my team is ready to storm that underground facility. Just give us a location."

There was a long pause before Jim's voice came back, colder this time. "My wife is not doing that. She's a mother, and she's not working in the field anymore."

Annabelle leaned in, her face glowing in the screen's light, eyes narrowed. Cory shifted beside me, his body suddenly tense, like he was trying to hear every word.

Maryanne cut in, her tone all business. "Jim, if we go into that underground facility, none of the comms will work. Whoever goes in needs to be prepared to go it alone."

Then, over the crackling line, I heard Theo muttering to Vivian, his words just a low rumble. "The EREBUS is more than just a code name. If we're right, it's a failsafe. We need to understand what it actually is before we make a move."

Through the static came a chair scrape, quick steps, and a door click—someone bailed while the others kept talking.

Cory leaned in even further, his eyes locked on the screen like he was trying to pull the words out of the air. I felt a chill creep down my spine. Cory was usually the first to crack a joke or throw out some sarcastic comment, but now he was stone silent, every muscle in his body coiled tight. I'd have to keep an eye on him.

Vivian's voice came through, calmer, more calculated. "Agreed. We can't afford to rush in blind. We need intel, not just brute force."

The voices overlapped, the adults talking over each other, their panic building like a pressure cooker about to blow. Then Reggie's voice cut through the chaos, rough and choked.

"This is all my fault. The teens wouldn't have been kidnapped if I'd seen the signs earlier."

There was a long silence, the kind that presses against your eardrums and makes your heart thud in your chest.

Jim's voice softened, but I could still hear the edge of frustration. "No one is blaming you, Reggie. We all missed it. But we can't miss the next move. We need to be smart. We need to be ready."

The line crackled again, then the background noise shifted. I heard the sound of a chair scraping back, footsteps shuffling, and then the door to my room creaked open.

Theo stepped in, his preppy polo and crisp khakis as out of place in my tense, teen-packed room as a yacht in floodwater. He paused, his hand still on the doorknob, his eyes moving over the four of us like he was counting suspects in a police lineup.

"What are you four doing?"

Ezra slammed the laptop shut, his face a picture of exaggerated innocence. "Uh, just… you know, a little light hacking. Nothing illegal. Probably."

Annabelle stifled a nervous giggle, and Cory cleared his throat like he was about to give a speech. I just rolled my eyes, forcing a smile.

"Yeah," I added, leaning back casually against the headboard. "Ezra was just showing us how to delete our embarrassing search histories. You'd be amazed what he can find with a few keystrokes."

Theo's eyes narrowed, his gaze flicking between us like he was trying to read a particularly tricky cipher. I held my breath, willing my face to stay neutral.

After a long, uncomfortable pause, he just sighed and turned to leave, his boat shoes making a soft thud against the hallway tiles as he muttered something about "kids these days" under his breath.

As soon as he was gone, Ezra slowly lifted the laptop lid again, his fingers hovering over the trackpad.

I let out a long breath, the knot in my chest loosening just enough to start breathing like a semi-functional human again. Then I glanced at Cory. His jaw was tight, his eyes too focused—like he wasn't just watching the screen, he was calculating. Something about him buzzed wrong. And I'd just started to think I could trust him.

MISSION: IMPROBABLE – FLIRTING WITH FIREWALLS AND UNDERGROUND BLUEPRINTS

"THAT WAS CLOSE," Ezra said as he typed on his laptop. "Sounds like the meeting is over." He snapped it shut for the second time.

"So what's the plan?" Annabelle asked.

"If only Kat had shared where the underground training facility was…" I paused before finishing. "Can you find that out, Ezra?"

He scratched his head. "Me? How?"

"Maryanne," I finished and patted him on the shoulder.

Ezra looked confused. "I can't hack her system."

"I think she meant, hack her," Annabelle explained. "Like sweet-talk her and tell her how awesome she is."

"And you think she'll just tell me where it is?"

I smiled my best Maryanne smile and flipped my hair. "No, I think she'll trust you enough to leave you alone with her computer."

"Don't you think that's something I should do?" Cory asked as he flexed a bicep. "I mean, come on, he might have pretty blue eyes but I've got all this and a face that makes people forget their own names."

Annabelle put both hands on her hips. "And what are you going to do with her computer? Flirt with it?"

"No, I'll give it to Ezra."

"I like it. A team effort," I said. If we didn't come up with some sort of plan and implement it right away, we'd end up arguing like the adults and getting nowhere. I paused and thought maybe there were a few adults we could get on our side.

"What was Reggie like before the teens were kidnapped," I glanced at Ezra's legs, "and the last failed mission?"

"He was awesome. Always upbeat. Like he ran this place. He didn't second-guess himself or ask for outside help," Cory said.

"Yep, he was on the ball. In fact, he advised Theo not to send me on the mission. I'm more of a tech person."

"Really," Annabelle scoffed.

"And Theo ignored him. Reggie hasn't been the same since then."

So one adult we could count on.

"Let's get that Reggie back."

I replayed the meeting in my head:

Adelina's voice cut in, sharp and clear: "Then why haven't you sent Ellie in yet? She's ready."

Father Raphael's deep, reassuring voice followed: "I agree. She's had the best training, and she's the only one young enough to blend in with those kids."

Two more adults we could count on. And possibly Lassiter and his team. He was ready to storm the training center.

I could talk to them, feel them out before I committed to telling them our plan.

"What is our plan?" Annabelle asked, interrupting my thoughts.

"Let Ezra and Cory find out where The Alliance Training Center is. You and I can talk to Adelina, Father Raphael, and Lassiter."

"That's really not his name," Annabelle reminded me.

"I know, but that's what I've been calling him in my head. Anyway, he's the one who got the intel that The Alliance was coming for me."

"And nobody has said anything about the fact they already tried to kill you on the highway," Ezra added. Then he turned to Cory. "Get your flirt on and let's go talk to Maryanne."

Cory struck a pose and Ezra shook his head in mock disgust.

"Let's do this thing," Cory added. "We should find out where the EREBUS is too."

"Why?" I said. "Surely, Agent Jim has it now."

"So Ezra can figure out *exactly* what it does." Cory opened the door and waved Ezra through first. "After you, my computer genius. Brawn follows brains."

Annabelle caught the door handle. "I don't think that's how the saying goes."

"I'm ready." I followed her out.

Cory and Ezra took the elevator while Annabelle and I opted for the stairs.

"So, if you don't mind me asking, what did your mom say?"

"She said she sent me here to protect me."

"And you believe her?"

"When has my mother ever told me the truth?"

I ran down the stairs, putting an end to the conversation.

Lassiter was standing in the hallway outside the meeting room whispering with Adelina and Father Raphael.

"Just the people I wanted to see," I whispered.

"Is there somewhere we can talk in private?" Annabelle asked.

"There's no one in the briefing room."

I almost said it was bugged. But Ezra bugged it. If they weren't on our side, it would give us away and they would de-bug it.

Once we were all in the briefing room,Lassiter closed the door and waited for me to speak.

"I'm ready to go undercover."

"Yeah, all we have done is go on training missions for pretend spies," Annabelle moaned.

"I agree," Adelina said. "We're wasting time."

"Everyone is more worried about the EREBUS than the teens," Lassiter said. "I say we go in, grab the teens, no matter what Joan and the rest of the team say."

"But we need to have a good plan," Kat said from behind me.

"What about Jim?" I asked.

"I won't go with you. Besides, Jim is like this on every mission."

I put my hand over my mouth, realizing I'd said more than I should have about Jim. Hopefully, she thought I was referring to the conversation in the car, not the one we'd heard through bugging the briefing room.

"I told Maryanne to give you the blueprints for the underground training facility America's Future used. We just need to find the new entrance."

"And let the adult agents be in charge," Father Raphael added. "I don't want to be responsible for more teens…"

He didn't finish the sentence because he didn't have to. My Shawn and Gus-saturated brain came up with a few witty retorts, but I'd learned enough in the past few days to keep those to myself right now.

Instead, I said, "What about Reggie?"

"What about me?" He suddenly appeared, and then closed a wall. A hidden door. Cool.

"Can you help us plan a mission to get the teens back?"

"You look like her, you know."

"My mother?"

"Yes, I trained her. She had the same amount of gumption you do."

I tried using a version of what my mother had said to our advantage. "She sent me here on purpose, you know."

"Sounds like the old her, before…"

"Before something bad happened?" I had no idea what he was talking about, but I thought I'd ride the get-Reggie-on-our-side wave.

"Yes, your father."

"My father left us." I stomped one foot and balled my fists at my side.

"Is that what she told you?" Reggie hung his head and ran a hand through his silver hair. "Your father was killed on a mission, right after you were born."

"That's why she got out," I finished for him. "Just another lie."

"To protect you, I'm sure." Father Raphael patted me on the back.

"I'm done with lies. They don't protect me." I

turned and ran out of the briefing room, my plans to rescue the world—or at least the teens—vanished in a puff of putrid deception.

I ran blindly up the stairs, tears streaming down my face. In my room, I wrestled my clothes off and my bathing suit on. I needed to swim away from the grief, the lies, and mourn the father I never knew.

I swam at the bottom of the pool, letting the water surround me and drown out the world. I came up for breath and dove again to swim the length of the pool. Back and forth until I couldn't swim another stroke. I came up panting and pounded my fists on the concrete until small drops of blood seeped into the water puddled at the edge.

"You are one of us," Annabelle said as she plopped into the water in a hot pink swimsuit.

"What?"

"I remember my first day here. There were all these teens, not like the three there were when you came." She frowned and took a deep breath. "I set my garbage bag down in the foyer and ten of them walked by in those snooty prep-kid uniforms… they were laughing… I thought…"

"I don't belong here," I finished for her. "That's what I said to myself my first day here. I'm not a foster kid."

"I thought I didn't belong here because I *was* a foster kid."

"That's funny."

"Yeah, the truth is, you belong more than I do. Your whole family is… was…spies. Even your godmother." She sunk under the water for a moment, coming up with a burst of bubbles.

"I was like a fish out of water here. My parents were drug addicts. They didn't get married. They didn't want me. So they left me at one of those drop boxes for babies."

"Oh…" I didn't know how to respond.

"But you are a fish in water. This is where you belong. I know you're upset your mom lied to you about your dad. But you have a mom who loves you. You had a dad who loved you."

"What am I supposed to do about all the lies? I don't feel like I can move forward."

She ignored my question and continued. "Reggie took me in after I'd been kicked out of ten foster homes." She ran her fingers through her fuchsia hair. "I can be a little dramatic and I don't like people controlling me."

"Like Shawn from *Psych*," I answered.

"But Reggie gave me a place. I'd just started my training when the mission went south and Ezra lost half his legs, and Cheyenne was killed."

"That's horrible, but aren't we just continuing the killing and the lies if we remain spies?"

"Look at you, being all rhyme-y. No. Don't you get it? You can save the thirty teens and get Reggie's mojo back. If he gets his mojo back, he can keep giving teens a family and a purpose."

"Or they can get injured or killed."

"Or overdose or get trafficked."

"What?"

"Don't you get it? That's what happens to foster teens. I'd rather die doing good than be trafficked or sucked into The Alliance."

I jumped back into the pool and washed the dried blood off my hands.

"I guess I've had a pretty good life. But I'm still mad at my mom for all the lies."

"You can totally be mad at her. But later. Let's go rescue those teens."

"I'm in. Race you to the other side."

Before she could answer, I dolphin-dove under and kicked my way to the other side. When I came up, she was drying herself with a towel.

"I don't know how to swim like that. Maybe you can teach me. Later. You need to dry off and we need to finish our plan." She strutted away from the pool edge. "Just so you know… this is the last one of these little open-heart chats we are ever going to have."

CHAPTER
EIGHTEEN

MISSION: HIJACKED – WELCOME TO THE SKETCHY BASEMENT OF DOOM

AFTER TOWELING OFF, I dusted my feet off before cramming them into wet soccer sandals.

I squelched my way up to the back door. Once inside, I decided to go check out the old wing and the unused computer lab. Maybe I'd find a clue to what EREBUS did or why it was there.

I set my soggy towel down on a pleather chair and began my search. I found some footprints on the dusty floor. Some of them were from us teens, left during the scavenger hunt. Others were older and covered with a layer of dust. One fresh set on top of both sets interested me. I glanced behind me and realized I was ruining clues with my wet soccer sandals. I reached for a chair on wheels and threw myself on, stomach first. This way, I could examine the footprints without creating any new ones.

The newest set reminded me of something I'd just seen—or heard, more like. It was the way the footprint displayed, a hard smudge in the heel and a lighter touch in the toe. The way Theo walked. I reached out a hand and pulled myself forward with the help of a table leg.

"What in the world are you doing?" Annabelle said as she jogged the four steps it took her to get to me. I reached out and punched her stomach, sending her into the seated position in a chair behind her.

"You're ruining evidence," I said as she huffed in disgust.

"I was looking for you because I can't find anyone. Like Brightwood is a ghost town."

Before I answered her, I propelled myself to the door before closing it. It locked with an ominous click.

"Great, now we are locked in here."

I held a finger to my lips before whispering, "I think I know who was after the EREBUS."

"The Alliance?"

"Yes, but someone working as a mole for The Alliance. Someone who could hand over thirty teens and no one would suspect." I wheeled myself close enough to her so that my face was facing her knees.

"Reggie?" she asked.

"No. Look at these shoe prints. Those are the fancy boat shoes Theo wears."

"Theo is the mole?" she gasped before grabbing my elbow. "Sit up. I'm tired of talking to your hair."

I flipped my body around and landed on my butt.

"I think Theo not only helped The Alliance kidnap the teens, but also has had his hand in everything since then. The scavenger hunt..."

"The fake missions. You and Agent Kat being run off the road in the woods..."

"You're a better agent than you give yourself credit for."

She smiled and crossed her legs. "So what are we going to do?"

"Well, first we find out if Brightwood is under attack."

"What?"

I opened my mouth to respond—but something was off.

A hum. Faint. Mechanical. Somewhere beyond the walls, something powered up. Lights didn't flicker. No alarms. But the temperature seemed to drop an inch.

My instincts snapped to high alert.

Beside me, Annabelle sat frozen in one of the dusty rolling chairs, her fingers locked around the armrests like they might sprout rockets and take her somewhere safer. I was in the twin chair—just as squeaky, just as useless in a crisis.

That's when I heard them:

Clack-thud. Clack-thud.

Not sneakers. Not dress shoes. Boots. Heavy. Fast. Like someone chasing something they didn't want getting away.

The sound echoed off the concrete walls, louder with each stride.

The boots stopped at the door. Someone punched in a code and the keypad beeped, signaling the user had gotten it wrong. After three more attempts and no success, the user hit the door with a fist.

"Let's go. We have what we came for, the EREBUS."

"You don't think they're hiding in there?" a deep, gruff voice answered.

"They wouldn't hide in there. It's a dusty old computer lab."

Was that Cory's voice? Maybe I'd gotten it all wrong. Maybe it wasn't Theo, but Cory all along. I held my breath until the boots tromped down the hallway. Annabelle and I sucked in a deep breath in unison, neither of us daring to move yet. How many seconds were we supposed to wait? If we moved too soon, they might double back and find us here.

If it *was* Cory... we weren't just dealing with a mole. We were trapped.

We stared at each other in wide-eyed terror, not sure how long to stay frozen. After counting to sixty without hearing another sound, I exhaled and coughed at the same time. The mold-covered dust was getting to me, and that was the least of my worries.

"Guys, it's me. Cory. I really messed up. What's the code? I need to come in."

My eyes widened. Could we trust him?

Before I could answer the question about trust, Annabelle was on her feet.

"Cory, I can't believe you. You are helping The Alliance. There is no way on God's green earth we are letting you in."

"Guys, Ellie, talk some sense into her, please."

"What sort of sense is that, Cory?" I stood, careful not to mess up the evidence of Theo's footprints. With both hands on the handle of the door, I continued, "The sense where I tell you the code and then you call for The Alliance soldiers down the hall?"

"Listen, I'll be honest with you. They are coming back. That's why I need to get you to safety."

"Yeah, not happening," Annabelle said as she pushed her chair in front of the door. I guess now was not the time to tell her the door swings out and not in.

"I don't trust you, Cory."

Mentally I rehearsed all the reasons I didn't trust him. Sure, he played the dumb good-looking guy. The brawn—wasn't that what he said? He had more brains than we gave him credit for. He could, and probably would, call the soldiers back at any moment. Sure, we weren't giving him the code, but if we didn't find another way out of this room, we were sitting ducks. They'd find a way to bypass the code or break the door down.

Forgetting about preserving the evidence, I walked around the edges of the lab, looking for a way out.

"Keep talking to him," I hissed as I felt for a hidden panel.

"I really liked you, Cory, and I thought you liked me," Annabelle said, complete with an emotional quiver in her voice.

He smacked the door with his fist. "I like you too, Annabelle. I told you I messed up. I want to fix this."

"What about earlier when you were flirting with Ellie when she was in the bathtub?"

"I was playing the part."

I couldn't resist. "Which part was that, Cory? The playboy? Or the trafficker?"

"Trafficker? What? Noooo. I would never…" A soft thud on the door. "Guys, they promised me things. Like I'd be a top agent."

The soft thud—which I guessed was his head against the door—landed at the perfect time. I found a panel and pushed it, and it clicked at the same time as his head hitting the door. The panel opened to a narrow hallway. I didn't know exactly where it went, but I had a feeling it went outside. I motioned to Annabelle, who ended the conversation with Cory by saying, "We don't trust you and we aren't coming out."

We slipped through the hidden panel, and it clicked shut behind us. I guess there was no going back.

The hallway zigzagged until it ended with a metal doorway. As much as I wanted to push it full force, I didn't. Cory and the soldiers could be waiting on the other side. I turned the knob, and it creaked as if I'd stepped on a dying mouse. So much for being quiet.

I opened the door a crack and peeked out. The row of pine trees that separated the main house from the pool house greeted me. No one had trimmed them for a long time, so the needles poked me in the face and hugged the stone on the mansion. I slipped out and felt my way to the left. If I was guessing correctly, we'd come out near the back door I had used to get to the pool.

Annabelle squished her way out beside me.

"Wrap your towel around your face," I commanded.

We both did, ending the pine needle assault on our faces. I was right. As I neared the end of the trees lining the mansion, I spotted the back doors. I stuck a foot out and then peered around the trees. It felt good to breathe fresh air, not saturated with mold and dust, or pine-scented. After I was sure the coast was clear, I stepped out. Annabelle stumbled out after me, and we both blinked in the bright sunlight.

"Told you I'd lure them out," Cory said from behind a bush.

Before we could turn, the back doors to the mansion burst open behind us. Alliance soldiers stormed out, fanning around us like a net snapping shut.

There was no escape.

Annabelle was having none of it. She lunged at Cory, pounded her fists on his chest, and screamed, "You traitor!"

Cory grabbed her and held her by the wrists before letting her go.

She tumbled back and rejoined me.

"Take them," Cory ordered.

The Alliance soldiers wasted no time snatching us and throwing us in the back of a van. Black carpet fibers went up my nose, and I sneezed. As Annabelle said, "God bless you," loudly, she shoved something in my hand.

I couldn't look at it or the soldiers would notice. Instead, I felt it. An earbud.

What was going on?

I pretended to brush my hair out of my eyes and shifted it into my ear.

Two Alliance soldiers climbed in the back with us, each holding a scary-looking rifle I couldn't name if my life depended on it. Long, matte black, with too many attachments—like they'd been built to star in an action movie and actually knew how to shoot without missing. One had a scope. The other had something that looked like a flashlight but definitely wasn't.

"About time," Ezra said in my ear. "Cory was trying to… never mind."

There was no answering him right now. I leaned back against the edge of the van and listened. I caught Annabelle's eye for a moment, and it was obvious by her expression—she had an earbud in too.

"The plan is for you three to infiltrate The Alliance, find the teens, take back the EREBUS, and escape."

Easy peasy. We didn't have to find the underground training facility. Check that off our to-do list. Now all we had to do was find the teens, grab the EREBUS, and escape. Oh, and figure out if Theo was the mole. Or Cory. Or both.

———

The van bumped along back streets before it descended down a tunnel. The two guards each pulled black cloths out of their pockets and put them over our heads. Then they zip-tied our hands behind our backs.

"No funny business," one of them ordered.

Ezra had gone silent. Either we'd lost him or he wasn't taking any chances by talking in our ears.

We continued to go down.

I'd done exercises like this with my mom: A hood over me. Eyes closed. *Use your sense of direction, Ellie.* Mom would command. After a few miles of running, her dragging me along, she'd stop, take the hood off, and ask me to draw a map.

That's exactly what I'd do when we stopped—if I could get a pen and paper. Otherwise, I'd have to draw it in my head.

We continued down for a few more minutes. The air smelled damp. The driver stopped.

"Nice to see you, Drake. You don't get down here much anymore."

"Nope, most of my missions are above ground." He laughed.

A series of beeps and the creaking of a gate opening, and we climbed down even further before coming to a crisp stop.

"All right, you two, let's go," said one of our captors.

He grabbed my elbow and led me to the edge of the van. I stepped down with his guidance and hit pavement, jarring my foot and sending my soccer sandal flying.

"Guys, I think you can take the hoods off now," Cory's voice said.

"Here's your sandal, Ellie." He shoved it on my foot.

"Not until we get inside the facility," the same soldier said.

I limped along slowly, pretending my foot was really hurt. It wasn't, but the more time it took us to get to the facility, the more time I had to use my five senses and think. There was a strong smell of oil—not super helpful. That was common in every parking garage, not just underground secret training facility parking.

We must have arrived at a door because our procession halted and someone typed in an eight-digit code. No use trying to remember the code. I wasn't trained to recognize the pitch of each number. The door swung open and we were dragged inside.

Our hoods were removed. I waited for my eyes to adjust to the fluorescent lights above us, glaring off the marble tile floors below.

"What are we supposed to do with these kids?" Drake asked. "I'd like to be above ground. This place gives me the willies."

"Our orders were to deliver them, that's all I know," one soldier said. He held up a hard case. "And this."

"I can take it from here, guys," Cory suggested as he reached for the case.

"Fine by me," Drake said. "Give the kid the case and let's get out of here."

Within ten seconds, we were alone in the hallway. Cory held the case and grinned.

"We got it."

"Now what?" Annabelle hissed.

"Let's go get the teens," I answered.

Cory held out a hand. "Comms first. They don't work down here anyway."

He pulled a small knife from his belt and sliced through the zip ties on our wrists—clean, efficient, like he'd done it a hundred times. My arms ached from being restrained, but I didn't say anything.

We both yanked the comms from our ears and shoved them into his hand.

I wasn't sure I trusted him. Actually, scratch that —I trusted him less with every breath. He'd said, *"Told you I'd lure them out,"* and—well—he had. Now we were trapped in The Alliance Training Center, he had the EREBUS, and we had no way to reach Ezra or the rest of the team. Zero contact. Zero backup. Zero clue what his game really was.

What could go wrong?

CHAPTER
NINETEEN

WELCOME TO THE BIG LEAGUES (WHERE YOU STILL GET STABBED WITH A FORK)

CORY LED us down the hallway. A few of the fluorescent bulbs flickered overhead, casting jump-scare shadows across the floor.

All I could think of was that *Psych* episode, "In Plain Fright," where Shawn and Gus go through a haunted house and end up catching an actual killer. Classic fake scares covering up a real crime.

And here we were, following Cory—potential traitor of the year—into The Alliance's Training Center. No backup. No comms. Just bad lighting and worse instincts.

Stop it, Ellie. What would Shawn do? He'd observe. Gus would panic and scream. I felt like doing both.

Annabelle nudged me and whispered, "Are we really doing this?"

I didn't answer. I mean, what choice did we have? After another ten seconds, the hallway opened into a large, brightly lit room with stations. Teens wearing uniforms typed on computers while others trained with boxing gloves. Still others fiddled with weapons, taking them apart and putting them back together.

Annabelle nudged me. "There's Cora. She was a Brightwood teen."

"Wave and smile," I commanded.

"What?"

"Remember the thing you are good at? Standing out or whatever you say."

"Yep."

"This is the time to use it. You want these teens to trust you. Act like you belong!"

She waved at Cora and then a few other teens and smiled.

"You too," she said.

"No. They don't know me. I'm just going to blend in, stick by you, and find out all the information I can."

Cory led us to a glass-walled office and knocked, which seemed redundant because the man inside, wearing the slim tailored suit, could see us. He waved us in and stood, smoothing his black hair with both hands. "Cory, good job. I'll take the device."

Cory grinned and handed him the case with the EREBUS inside.

The slick-haired man set it down and motioned to two chairs. "I've been reading your files, Annabelle and Ellie. Interesting stuff."

He flipped through some papers with my name across the top. I knew he said "interesting stuff" meaning my file was pretty weird.

"Ellie, you have some skills we don't normally see here."

I'm sure he meant living off the grid, but I had no intention of discussing my training with him. I'd barely been able to digest the fact that my mother had trained me to be a spy.

I swiveled my head around his office. "Where exactly is "here"? Some off-the-grid bunker for trafficking teens?"

I gave a sideways glance at Annabelle after she stomped on my toes. She looked as if she had swallowed too much water in the pool. We were at a disadvantage because not only were we in an underground training center for The Alliance, we were still in our bathing suits, and the air down here was cold. Frosty.

"Let's not get off on the wrong foot here. Ellie, surely you know all these teens are foster kids and none of them are here under duress."

I looked at Annabelle again. She was under duress. But she'd transformed her waterlogged look into a plastic fake smile. She tilted her head sideways in a way that made her look cute and nonthreatening.

I couldn't look threatening either, with a soggy towel wrapped around me and hair I'm sure was sticking out in all directions.

"I'm glad we are here," Annabelle said, saving us from me getting us killed, I'm sure. "I saw some of my friends out there."

I followed her lead to the best of my ability and changed gears. "So do you think we could change out of these wet things?"

Her little sideways smile worked.

"Of course." He stood and waved a teen inside the office. "See that these girls get some fresh clothes and show them to their accommodations."

The teen gave the man—whose name we still didn't know—a slight bow and waved us out the door. Annabelle led the way. The wrong way. He redirected her. "I'm Dean. I remember you, Annabelle, from Brightwood."

"Oh," she said.

I could practically see the gears in her head turning, trying to place him.

I intervened this time. "Hi, I'm Ellie. I'm new. I haven't met you yet. Tell me about yourself and…" I waved my arm around the room. "The Alliance Training Center," I added, trying out the name.

"Oh," he paused. "I guess I didn't think you'd

been briefed yet." He slipped his hands in his trouser pockets and took on more of a relaxed air.

"So as I said, I'm Dean. I'm twenty, so I'm being trained to be a full-time agent by the time I turn twenty-one in a few months."

"And you came from Brightwood Academy?" I asked as if it were the most natural question in the world.

"Yeah. Yeah. That's right. So you already know how this all works then."

Annabelle batted her eyelashes. "I don't. So can you explain it?"

He stopped at a door and punched in a code. I wasn't sure if I should follow him in, so I stopped. Annabelle did too.

"Oh, come on in. This is just a uniform supply closet."

And yet they kept it locked.

"Actually, you two know your sizes better than I could guess. Besides, I know what girls are like if you get them wrong."

I grabbed a pair of khakis in my size.

"Take two of those. And then you're going to need two polos." He pointed to forest green polos with the emblem *The Alliance* written in a circle. If we hadn't known before where we were, we did now.

Before we finished, we each had two gym uniforms, the khakis and polos for classroom learning, plaid skirts and blazers, swimsuits, goggles, and a bunch of other gear. As I balanced my stack, I gave Annabelle a swift kick in the behind.

"Oh, yes, can you explain everything to me?"

"Sure. Where were we?"

He stopped to fist bump another teen and say, "See you on the mat, bro. And you're going down."

We arrived at a hallway, and he punched in another code. "These are the girls' dorms. I'm not allowed back there. You two are roomies."

"How do we know which room?" I asked, trying to keep the conversation going.

"Hey Ronnie!" he yelled. "See you in a few. Ready to spar?"

And then he jogged after Ronnie.

I was holding the door, which was good because we needed to find our rooms. But bad for two reasons: One, we didn't get any more information out of Dean. Two, if we left the girls' dorms, there was no way to get back in without the code.

Annabelle led the way, checking each door until she found one with a sticky note with our names on it. She opened it, and we both dumped our clothes on the beds. The room consisted of two twin beds, two desks with no computers or phones, a mini fridge, a closet on either side, and a folder with our names for each of us. Printed under my name was the keycode for the girls' dorm. One mystery solved.

"I'm going to take a quick shower before I

change," Annabelle said. The bathroom was definitely a step down from the ones at Brightwood. No fancy tub or marble countertops. Just a small shower with a translucent curtain. A small vanity, which Annabelle would cover with her makeup and hair gadgets, if she had them.

She turned the water on in the shower and popped back out to say, "Look. Makeup and a curling iron."

"Listen, this isn't summer camp," I reminded her as I pulled a hanger out of my small closet. "We are here on a mission."

"Doesn't mean we can't look good," she called from the bathroom.

One of the major downers of showing up to a mission in a bathing suit—besides the zero gear and zero dignity—was that I couldn't use any tech. Like the bug-sweeper I'd used my first night at Brightwood.. I realized I should watch what I say.

A screen I hadn't noticed before came to life, and Cory's face appeared.

"I checked your room for slugs," he said and laughed at his own joke.

I pointed to the screen. "What is this?"

"It's like a telephone. The kind you pick up and dial."

Annabelle swished out of the bathroom wearing only a towel.

"No it's not, if you can see me, you perv." She

wrapped her towel tighter and moved away from the screen. "And stop making fun of my roomie and tell us what is going on."

"Not on the phone," I cautioned. "Meet us somewhere."

I didn't trust Cory as far as I could throw him. Rephrase that. I couldn't throw him at all. I didn't trust him as far as he could throw me. Which was pretty far.

"Let's meet after dinner, which is in half an hour."

"How do you know that?" Annabelle asked as she thrust her head into a polo.

"The schedule is in your folder."

I picked up the folder and pulled out the schedule.

"Meet me in the computer lab after dinner." The screen went black.

According to the schedule, dinner wear was a plaid skirt, polo, and blazer for the girls — not unlike the uniforms at Brightwood. I sensed a subtle tactic in the uniform, the schedule, the classes: Mimic Brightwood Academy. Do most things the exact same way so the teens felt as if they'd been chosen, not stolen or trafficked.

I showered next and asked Annabelle to do something with my hair, which meant I ended up with two fiery red pigtails on top of my head.

"I look like a cartoon," I complained.

"You look like a teen. You'll see."

When we walked into the cafeteria, I did see. The female teens had various shades of neon hair in pigtails, nubs, or beehived on top of their heads.

"They'd be so jealous if they knew this," she flipped a pigtail, "is your natural color."

Their eyes were lined heavily like Annabelle's, and encased in shades of bright blue, green, and an occasional orange.

Cora, the teen she'd greeted earlier, waved us over.

"This is Ellie," Annabelle introduced me as we slid into our seats.

"I don't remember you from Brightwood," Cora said. "Welcome to the big leagues."

"What does that mean?" Annabelle asked as she scrunched up her face the way she did when she was offended.

"Oh." She smacked Annabelle on the back. "I didn't mean anything by it. I just thought maybe Theo didn't graduate you because you weren't ready after… you know."

"I don't know. I'm new."

"And yet you got recruited right away." She smiled a crocodile sort of grin—the kind that makes you feel as if she would just as soon devour you as smile at you.

"So how did you get recruited?"

She straightened and pulled her shoulders back. "Theo said I'm the cream of the crop."

"I'm sure you are," I answered and stabbed my fork into my chicken breast, pretending it was her for Annabelle's sake. "I mean, how did they graduate you to the big leagues? Was there some sort of ceremony?" I picked up my knife and jabbed the meat.

Annabelle let out a snort and then covered her mouth.

"What's so funny?" Cora replied.

"Oh, you don't know." Annabelle smoothed her skirt. "Ellie here grew up off the grid. I don't think she knows the proper way to use utensils."

I knew the underlying meaning. I knew how to use a fork and knife as a weapon. Cora didn't catch the underlying meaning.

"Oh, you poor thing. They'll teach you here," she said in an exaggerated voice as if I were hard of hearing and stupid.

"Well, no, there was no ceremony." Cora turned to Annabelle and continued. "It was clandestine." She turned to me and explained, "Clandestine, Ellie, means secret—like, really secret. But not in your 'hide your snack stash under the bed' kind of way. It's more… refined. Think espionage, covert operations, or, I don't know… people who actually know how to keep a secret without telling their dog. It's French, obviously. Maybe you've heard of it in a book? No? Hmm. Shocking."

She turned back to Annabelle while I held my

knife up to her back and mimicked stabbing Cora, despite the seriousness of the situation.

"So Theo, and hey Cory," she puckered her lips at him as he joined us and leaned on the table, so he could flex and display his muscles.

"Don't forget, Annabelle, Ellie—meeting after dinner." He reached over and pried the knife out of my hand. "Glad to see you are making friends." He plunked it on the table.

Cora grasped his free arm. "I could come to a meeting with you, Cory."

Cory shook his arm free. "Maybe another night, gorgeous." He winked and trotted off like the handsome stallion that he knew he was.

"And sooo," Cora continued, as if she hadn't had a flirty break. "We were whisked off in the middle of the night and graduated to here." She waved a hand of hot pink painted nails around the cafeteria. "We've been training for new missions."

"What did Theo say about Brightwood?" I asked, forgetting she thought I was stupid.

She turned her attention to me, picked up her napkin and pulled a pen out of her blazer pocket. She drew what I think was a fish and then a house with columns that looked like Brightwood. "The Big Alliance swallowed up Brightwood, understand?" Then she made all sorts of hand motions I didn't understand.

Annabelle motioned at the clock, and I stood.

"She doesn't understand, does she?" Cora asked.

Cora patted me on my lower back. "Maybe they can use you as a janitor or something."

I reached for my knife, and Annabelle jogged around Cora to grab both my arms.

"Come on, Ellie. Let's go," she said in the same exaggerated voice Cora had just used with me.

SPY SCHOOL HEARTBREAK CLUB: WE FIGHT, WE FLIRT, WE MIGHT DIE

THE COMPUTER LAB was dark except for one blue-green screen with a shadowy form leaning over the keyboard.

"Ezra, you're here." I clapped my hands together. Then threw a hand to my lips.

This was a secret meeting. Yelling in jubilation that the guy you had a crush on was here was not clandestine.

I muffled a laugh, thinking about the way Cora had explained the word to me.

"Shut the door and lock it," Ezra commanded as he continued to type furiously on the keyboard.

"I'll pull the shades."

The room was centered in the main level of the training center with plexiglass walls, meaning anyone could see what was going on, including the slick-haired man, whose name I still didn't know. His office was glass, too. I got the purpose. The fishbowl effect. Everyone was being watched all the time.

As I closed the shades, I did a quick sweep of the main floor. No laser tripwires. No black-clad assassins rappelling from the rafters. Just Cory sulking in a corner and Ezra hacking something like it was a casual Tuesday. Good.

"I've been able to hide our activity here," Ezra said, finally looking up from his keyboard. "I hijacked their security system and spoofed it. As far as they know, the lab's empty."

Casual Tuesday confirmed.

That's when I noticed Cory. Head down. Hands gripping his hair like it might escape.

"Guys, I'm sorry," he mumbled.

Annabelle locked on like a missile. "You traitor!" She launched across the room and started smacking him in the head like a tiny, furious jackhammer.

"He was a traitor," Ezra said calmly. "He's not anymore."

Not anymore? That was like saying a tornado had been destructive but had recently taken up knitting. We were already deep in enemy territory—off the grid, out of contact, smack in the center of the dragon's lair. The kind of scenario my mom had trained me for since I was old enough to hold a fork and stab someone with it.

"Cory, you are a genius," I said, prying Annabelle off him like she was made of Velcro.

His head jerked up. "I am?"

"You fed thirty teens to The Alliance," Annabelle snapped. "And let the assassins—"

He sliced a finger across his throat in the international gesture for "oops, you were supposed to die."

"And I showed up," I said flatly.

He nodded. "Yeah. Then the FBI. You and Kat were supposed to be toast."

"This is officially the worst team meeting of my life," Annabelle muttered. "I'm going to my room to make my own plan—unless you explain yourself, Cory." She jabbed him in the chest. Then turned on me. "And you better explain why he's suddenly a genius."

I glanced between them. Annabelle's glare. Cory's pacing. Ezra's unreadable expression.

Honestly, she wasn't wrong. This meeting sucked. The only way it didn't end with one of us strangling the other was if I could convince them Cory hadn't just doomed us all with his bad choices—but had accidentally handed us a way out.

Cory ran a hand through his hair, looking like he wished it were a paper shredder.

"I went to the FBI," he said. "Told them everything. Not your godmother though, Ellie. She'd probably torture me."

Fair point. She probably would. I might even hold her purse.

"True. And then ask you what you learned from it," I said, grabbing a rolling chair and folding my legs underneath me like I was settling in for a TED Talk. Non-threatening posture engaged. Maybe Cory would stop looking like he'd just failed spy kindergarten.

"After I told them everything, I thought Agent Jim was going to toss me in a cell and throw away the key," Cory said.

"But Father Raphael disagreed?" I asked, flashing back to the weirdly serene priest by the pool. He had the kind of chill that made me wonder if it was the Holy Spirit... or the fact that he was definitely packing heat.

Cory flopped into another chair. "Yeah. So Kat and Adelina decided that getting us into The Alliance's underground training center was actually smart."

"And Ezra?" I asked, tilting my chin toward him.

"I told him everything too."

Awesome. So everyone got the classified memo except Annabelle and me. And while I could pretend that was fine—because, hi, lifelong outsider over here —Annabelle wasn't exactly known for her chill.

"You let us get taken… in our bathing suits," she snapped, crossing her arms tightly over her Alliance-issued uniform like it had personally betrayed her.

"It was perfect," I said. "And yeah, I'm mad you didn't tell us. But you set it up right. We're inside. And we're alive."

And if we were going to rescue the thirty teens, take back the EREBUS, and not end up as Alliance test subjects, Cory needed to get his act together. Fast. Because it wasn't going to be the agents who pulled this off—it was us. A bunch of teens who could blend in by standing out. Shawn Spencer would be proud.

Annabelle grabbed her hair like she was resisting the urge to scream. "You gave them the EREBUS?"

"No," Ezra said, his fingers flying across the keyboard. A 3D schematic lit up the screen like a sci-fi movie prop. "I created a decoy. What they have is a shell. Looks real, does nothing."

"They haven't figured that out yet?" I asked.

Cory shook his head. "No one down here knows what it actually does. They locked it in the vault like some priceless artifact."

"Which buys us time," Ezra added. "Top Alliance brass has a big meeting next week. That's when their lead scientist is supposed to examine it."

"How do you know that?" I asked.

Ezra and I answered in sync. "Theo."

Of course. More secrets. More planning. More of

Annabelle and me being left in the metaphorical—and literal—dark.

"I bugged all of Brightwood," Ezra said casually, like that was a totally normal hobby.

"You couldn't have told us?" Annabelle snapped, gesturing toward me like she was about to cross-examine him.

"No offense, Ellie," Ezra said, "but you're new. I didn't know if I could trust you."

Wow. Thanks for that.

"I had a reason to surveil Theo. I've already paid for this mission. With my legs." Ezra's voice was quiet, but it hit like a gut punch.

"And me?" Annabelle asked sharply.

Ezra faltered. His eyes flicked to mine. I knew that look. He needed a lifeline.

"She's a girl," I said, deadpan.

Cory nodded like a bobblehead.

"And apparently so am I," I added, eyebrows raised. "Which, surprise! Doesn't cancel out our ability to do spy things."

Ezra glanced away, cheeks faintly pink. "After what happened to Cheyenne, I couldn't let you two walk into the field and become the next casualties."

The lie hung in the air like fog. It wasn't about the girl. It was about control. And fear.

Annabelle looked ready to explode. Her face was as red as my hair. I imagined cartoon steam blasting from her ears.

Before she could launch into a full WWE take-down, I jumped out of my seat and leaned in close. "Let's prove them wrong."

Sure, I meant prove she's not a loose cannon. But proving girls belonged in this mission? That was the best place to start.

I steered her into my chair and turned back to the boys. "Now. Since you two masterminds have the blueprints, kindly loop us in."

Please, I begged silently, *let Cory pull it together.*

He stood. Hesitated. Then spoke. "The FBI wants us to gather intel. Learn how The Alliance operates and feed them information. There's an old mail chute we can send reports through."

I scratched my head. "And then what? The FBI swoops in like caped crusaders and saves the day?"

"Yes," Ezra said. "Recon only. Minimal risk."

"That's not gonna fly," I said, tugging the knot out of my ponytail. My hair fell into my face like a theater curtain: Scene Two—Ellie Has Concerns.

"Why not?" Cory asked.

"Because the teens don't think they're prisoners."

"Exactly," Annabelle said, nodding. "They think they're special. Like spy school elites. We're just the extras."

She pointed to each of us like she was making a case to a jury. Spoiler alert: the jury agreed.

"So what do we do?" Cory asked.

"Prove we're better," Annabelle said, standing and striking a power pose.

Ezra sighed. "No…"

I could see it in his eyes. He thought Annabelle was going to blow the whole thing. But maybe blowing it up was the only way forward.

"No, Ezra. She's right. We have to earn our place here."

"And we earn it by dominating," Annabelle said, raising a victorious fist.

"But you're only half-trained," Cory pointed out.

"Then we start tonight," I said. "Can we get into the training areas?"

Ezra grinned. "I can get us in anywhere."

"Great. Annabelle—let's suit up and show them what we're made of."

———

The training room at midnight was sterile and humming, lit by that special kind of fluorescent lighting that made everyone look vaguely like a villain. Ezra disabled the security feed in less than ten seconds, which was simultaneously impressive and terrifying.

"We've got two hours," he said, voice calm and crisp as always. "I looped the hallway cams and pinged a janitor bot to keep watch. If it sees anything weird, it'll send me a signal."

Ezra was born for the van. He was our guy in the chair—even without a van—and honestly, I wouldn't want him anywhere else. If I was going to throw punches and dodge whatever "surprises" this spy-lab had waiting, I wanted Ezra in my ear and Cory out of the way.

"Okay." I cracked my knuckles and stepped onto the mat. "Let's see if any of this actually stuck."

Cory leaned against the wall, arms crossed, clearly thinking I'd flail around and maybe twist an ankle. Poor boy.

Annabelle paced like a jungle cat, sizing up the room. Not joining in. Not yet.

I took a breath, letting Mom's voice play on loop in my head: *Stay centered. Know your exits. Never show weakness. And if all else fails, aim for the nose.*

Ezra called out commands like he was running a simulation. "Straight strikes. Low block. Turn. Duck—yep, duck faster."

"Was that slow?" I asked, panting.

"You duck like someone who's only seen it in movies," he deadpanned.

I shot him a glare sharp enough to count as a weapon.

But I was getting better. Faster. The movements were familiar now—not just in theory but in my *bones*. For the first time since arriving at Brightwood, I didn't feel like the new girl. I felt like a spy.

"Alright," Cory said, finally pushing off the wall. "My turn."

"Oh good," I muttered. "I've always wanted to legally punch someone I mildly dislike."

Cory grinned and stepped onto the mat. I feinted left, darted right, and aimed for a takedown.

He blocked me. Smugly.

"Not bad," he said.

"Don't patronize me," I snapped.

I lunged again, and this time got him off balance. But I didn't drop him. Yet.

Ezra whistled from his corner. "Okay, that was decent."

Annabelle still hadn't joined. She was watching. Analyzing. And maybe seething a little.

After another round, Cory clapped his hands. "Alright, pause. We've got another issue."

I wiped sweat from my neck. "Besides you being annoyingly hard to punch?"

He ignored me. "Some of the other girls—Alliance girls—are noticing I'm not paired off like the rest of the recruits. It's a thing here. Keeps eyes off you if you're in a couple. Less suspicion."

"And your solution is what?" Annabelle asked, eyes narrowed.

"I think we should pretend to be dating."

There was silence.

"Absolutely not," she snapped.

Cory blinked. "It's not real—"

"I know *that*, genius. But I don't *fake* stuff like that."

Her voice cracked just slightly at the end, and ohhh. Okay. Note to self: Annabelle might *actually* like him. File under: Complicated.

"Then what about you two?" Cory turned to Ezra and me. "If she won't do it, maybe Ellie will be your fake girlfriend."

I tilted my head. "Are you offering me a fake relationship? Because I feel like I should've been warned with a PowerPoint or at least a pros and cons list."

Ezra coughed. "Strategically, it makes sense. We're often together. You can sit with me at meals. It wouldn't be hard to sell."

"Exactly," Cory said. "Which gives me a reason to talk to her and the rest of you guys without it looking suspicious.

I glanced at him. He didn't look smug. He didn't look hopeful. He looked… nervous. Which weirdly made me feel a tiny bit brave.

"I'm in," I said, before I could overthink it.

Annabelle's eyebrows shot up so high they practically left her face. "You're serious?"

"Look," I said, "we're not exactly running a normal op. If fake-dating Ezra keeps us under the radar, great. If it gets us extra mashed potatoes at dinner? Even better."

Ezra blinked. "That's… fair."

Cory, still awkward, gave a nod. "Cool. We'll keep it casual. Just enough to deflect attention."

"Can we get back to training now?" Annabelle huffed.

Cory stepped onto the mat. "Come on then. You think you can take me?"

That's when she smiled. The kind of smile that made me instinctively step back and consider writing my will.

"I know I can."

She moved like lightning. No warning. No warm-up. One moment, Cory was upright. The next, he was flat on his back, blinking at the ceiling.

"Ow," he muttered.

"Surprise," she said, offering him a hand.

"You've been training."

I should've guessed—Annabelle had been holding back during our sparring sessions, playing the wide-eyed recruit while secretly running a midnight ninja program on herself.

"Every night since that mission. After what happened to… her." She looked away. "I didn't want to be the girl who froze again."

Ezra's voice was soft. "You didn't freeze. No one saw that coming."

"Yeah, well. Never again."

We gathered our gear, adrenaline still buzzing in my ears as we slipped into the corridor, trying to act like four totally normal teens who *definitely* hadn't just faked a bunch of romantic relationships and nearly broken each other's noses.

That's when Annabelle spotted it. A small metal panel, old and rusted, tucked low into the wall.

"There," she said. "Is that the chute?"

Cory crouched. "Yeah. It's the mail chute. We can test it tomorrow."

I was about to respond when a smooth, too-casual voice echoed from behind us.

"Well, well," said Theo. "What are the four of you doing out past curfew?"

We froze.

Ezra's fingers twitched near his pocket, probably reaching for whatever gadget could save us.

I reacted first.

"We were... talking," I said, stepping closer to Ezra and looping my arm through his. "Needed some air. Couple stuff."

Cory glanced at Annabelle and took the risk. He slid his arm across her shoulders. "We had a… disagreement."

Annabelle didn't punch him. A miracle.

Theo's eyes narrowed, lingering just a second too long on the mail chute behind us.

"You're lucky I enjoy teenage drama," he said, voice velvet with menace. "But next time, save the romance for daylight hours."

He turned on his heel and walked off.

We didn't move until the hallway lights buzzed again.

"He saw the chute," I whispered.

Ezra nodded grimly. "We need to use it. Now. Before he figures out what we're planning."

I met his eyes.

For the first time, I didn't feel like I was pretending to be a spy.

I *was* one.

And now… we were officially out of time.

SPY GAMES AND SKITTLES-TONED SABOTAGE

AFTER LAST NIGHT'S close call with Theo, I knew we didn't have long to test the old mail chute. The only problem? We had nothing to send—and just an hour before breakfast to find something.

Going to bed at 2:30 a.m. punched me straight in the face when the alarm blared at 5:30. Annabelle and I had agreed to get up early and go to the gym.

"That's what girls do," she'd said, like it explained everything.

Personally, I'd rather be in the woods with a Yeti full of hot chocolate, waiting for the sun to rise. Turns out, teen girls don't stalk turkeys—they stalk each other. Same principle. You hunt to prove your skill. In the woods, you bring home dinner. In the teen world, you bring down your opponent and brag about it in the dining hall.

Annabelle had already laid out my gym clothes. If it were up to me, I'd have thrown on my mom's old gray sweats and an oversized T-shirt. But nope. She'd pulled my official Alliance-issued gear: hunter-green, high-waisted leggings and a matching sports bra.

"Where's the shirt?" I asked as she shimmied into a neon-pink pair of leggings, same make and model.

She lightly punched me in the ghost-white stretch of my exposed stomach. "You're so silly. You don't wear a shirt. Now flex those abs and show me what you've got."

I flexed. My abs rippled for maybe a second before giving up.

"Keep flexing," she ordered, wrestling her sports bra on. Once it was in place, she demonstrated with a flawless six-pack.

"We have to stay flexed the whole time?"

"Only when other girls are around." She grabbed our water bottles, tearing a lemon-lime hydrate packet from the shelf. "Drink up."

"I thought we were supposed to find intel to send through the mail chute."

"We are. But Ellie, you're on different turf now. You're not stalking a buck. You're stalking teen girls. And there's no bow and arrow."

I filled my bottle under the faucet, capped it, and gave it a good shake. So, not *too* different from the woods—just shinier, sneakier, and with more eyeliner.

"What we're going to do," she said, "is survey the gym."

"You mean there'll be people there this early?"

"Not people. Teen girls," she replied, slinging her gym bag over her shoulder. I followed her out the door.

Since real-life stalking, spying, and social survival were all new to me, I wasn't sure what to say in the hallway. Was someone listening? Ezra, definitely. Cameras? Probably. Mail chute infiltration? Off-limits in conversation. So I kept quiet and let Annabelle lead.

"When we get in there," she explained, "look around. Spot the queen bees."

"Like Cora?"

She grinned. "You catch on quick. Just… no stabbing her with a butter knife."

"Maybe I should stick close to her. She still thinks I'm deaf and dumb."

"Great idea."

We turned the corner toward the gym, and sure enough, Annabelle had been right. The place was packed. Girls in every neon variation of our Alliance gear filled the room—pink, yellow, orange. And here's the kicker: they were all wearing makeup. Like, *full-blown, YouTube-influencer-ready makeup.*

Annabelle reached over and manually closed my

gaping mouth with one hand while opening the door with the other.

"Told you," she whispered.

We passed treadmills, rowing machines, stationary bikes, and a section where girls did Pilates or lifted weights. We stashed our bags and joined the crowd.

Cora, of course, had a whole flock around her—every one of them dressed like a Skittles commercial. Her laser-green eyes locked on me and went wide with recognition.

"Oh girls, this is the new recruit I was telling you about," she said, lips pinked and voice syrupy sweet, like I was a toddler with an ear infection.

Her group parted like the Red Sea, and she gestured to the treadmill next to her.

"Let me show you how this works," she said slowly, enunciating each word. "This is a treadmill."

Then, to the girl in yellow she said, "She grew up in the *woods*. Off the *grid*."

Yellow-girl gasped dramatically. And at that exact moment, the treadmill started—fast. I barely caught myself, grabbing the rails with both hands as my feet flew behind me. Right before my nose met the display screen, I recovered and jogged into rhythm.

"There you go," Cora said, a condescending smile in full bloom. "You got it."

I wasn't sure if she'd jacked up the speed on purpose to humiliate me or had been too busy whispering to Lemon-Pants. But this wasn't a turkey hunt —this was a full-blown teenage jungle. And turkeys, for all their strutting, never tried to manipulate you into public humiliation just to secure their spot as queen.

I kept jogging. Not because I needed to, but because that's what Mom and Joan had drilled into me since I could walk. I stayed in character, flexed my abs, and kept my expression blank. I wasn't just invisible. I was *observing*.

"So yeah," Cora said, loudly. "Ellie here just got in yesterday. Maybe she'll end up working maintenance or something…"

She trailed off and stopped her treadmill. "Have you heard about the new mission?"

I leaned slightly toward her, stumbling just enough to play clueless.

"Yeah," she said louder, like she wanted *everyone* to hear. "Only the ones who pass the test this afternoon will be chosen for the mission."

Lemon-Pants perked up. "What mission?"

"Oh, I don't know," Cora said with fake innocence. "Only the top agents are going. You don't get the details until you pass."

"What test? When is it?"

"If you didn't get an invite in your inbox, you're not in," Cora said, pressing a button to increase her treadmill's speed. "Gotta train."

She waved her posse off and popped earbuds in.

I jogged five more minutes to stay in character, then hit the red button. The treadmill jolted as it stopped, launching me slightly forward. I caught myself with one hand, gave Cora a sheepish grimace, and hopped off.

She hit me with a *you-poor-thing* look that made me want to bench-press her face.

I found Annabelle by the water station.

"I've got nothing," I whispered. "No intel to send. Just gossip and the name of a test I'm not invited to."

She shook her head. "Same. Except now I know Cora's not the only one who wants in on the mission. The older Alliance girls—the ones here before Brightwood—they don't want us involved. At all."

"So we're the intruders."

"No. We're the *competition*."

We walked in silence toward the locker room, but I couldn't shake the feeling crawling up my spine.

We hadn't just walked into a spy academy.

We'd walked into enemy territory.

And I was pretty sure the first test had already begun.

The dining hall smelled like powdered eggs, disappointment, and exactly zero consequences for bad coffee.

Annabelle and I had arrived early—me still

mentally recovering from the gym's Hunger Games energy, and her looking like she'd just won it. We were in full Alliance uniforms: plaid skirts, crisp blouses, navy blazers. She carried herself like she hadn't just been fake-dating her almost-crush to get another girl off his case. I... was still trying to keep my abs flexed from earlier. Just in case.

Ezra and Cory wandered in ten minutes later, sleep-deprived and trayless. Ezra's hair looked like it had lost a fight with a pillow, and Cory had that glazed-over look of someone who'd just realized there was no time for breakfast or deodorant.

Just then Cora arrived in person, like the villain reveal in a teen drama no one asked for: Coral blazer, catwalk strut, and lips as glossy as her ego.

"Well *good morning*," she said, ignoring the rest of us as she leaned between Annabelle and Cory. "I didn't see you at the gym, Cory. Were you resting up for *me*?"

He straightened and didn't hesitate. "I was with my girlfriend."

Cora blinked. "You're what now?"

"Taken," he said, sliding an arm—smoothly this time—over Annabelle's shoulders. "Kind of into someone else."

Annabelle didn't even blink. "Private training session."

Cora's smile went tight, like she'd bitten into a lemon and tried to pretend it was cake. "How...

cute." She gave a little finger wave and sauntered off, hips swinging like a cartoon villain who didn't know the good guys were gaining on her.

Annabelle peeled Cory's arm off her shoulders. "Do that again without warning me and I'll break your elbow."

"Fair."

Ezra leaned in, voice low. "Okay. Focus. What did we get from the gym?"

"Cora mentioned a test this afternoon," I said. "Top-tier candidates only. No invite, no info. She made sure I knew I wasn't on the list."

"And then said you should probably mop floors," Annabelle added. "She's really branching out with her career advice."

Cory leaned forward. "We need to send something through the chute—today."

Ezra shook his head. "There's nothing solid to send. No names. No mission data. Just rumors."

"Exactly," I said. "So we make it *look* like a letter home. 'Hey Mom, there's a special test. Hope I get picked!'" I pointed at Ezra. "You encrypt the real message inside the phrasing. If Theo intercepts it, it reads like a homesick kid trying to earn brownie points."

Ezra tilted his head. "That could work."

"Give me something to write on," I said.

Cory pulled a sheet of paper from his blazer.

"This was going to be a fake quiz for cover. Use the back."

Annabelle had gone quiet. She pushed her half-eaten apple away and said, "I *want* to do the test but I don't think I'm the best candidate."

All eyes turned to her.

"I was at the gym this morning. I saw the girls who *are* getting invited. And yeah, I flipped Cory off guard last night, but that doesn't mean I'm ready. Ellie is. She's the only one here who didn't come in blind."

I looked at her. "Annabelle—"

"Nope. This is the part where I'm a good team player." Her voice dropped. "You're our best shot. Go win it."

Ezra pulled up something on his wrist device. "There's a slot. One girl dropped due to a knee injury. I can ghost Ellie into her place and reroute the e-vite."

"Do it," I said before I could second-guess myself.

Cory looked at me. "Once the invite goes out, you're on their radar."

"Good," I said, folding the letter and handing it back to him. "It's about time they started watching the right person."

Ezra nodded. "You'll get the e-vite by lunch. Play surprised."

I flexed my abs. "I'm already in character."

CHAPTER
TWENTY-TWO

SPY SCHOOL HUNGER GAMES – NOW WITH GLITTER

CORA'S LOOK when I announced at lunchtime to my little group that I'd received an e-vite to *The Test* could've curdled oat milk.

Cora froze mid-strut, lips parting in a perfect glossed "O" of disbelief—like the system had glitched and handed a golden ticket to the girl who, gasp, grew up without Wi-Fi and didn't even own a flat iron.

"Wait... *you* got in?" she asked, voice soaked in condescension and artificial peach.

I gave her my best blank blink. "Guess I'm not just here to mop floors."

Ezra coughed into his water. Annabelle didn't bother hiding her smirk. Cory muttered something like "Boom" into his protein bar.

I tucked the invitation slip—printed on faux-parchment, like spy school Hogwarts—back into my blazer pocket. If I played it cool, I'd look like I belonged. If I smiled too wide, I'd look like a tourist. If I passed out from nerves, I'd ruin the whole mission.

Balance, Ellie. Balance and flexed abs.

Across the room, Cora's loyal lemon-pants brigade was already whispering. I didn't need to hear the words to know they were plotting. I'd just flipped the social chessboard, and for once, I wasn't the pawn.

I'd made sure I announced it aloud while she was once again lingering at our table and making pouty lips at Cory, who had wrapped an arm around Annabelle's shoulders as proof they were fake-together. Annabelle had hiked an elbow up to jab him in the nose, when she'd caught my nod toward Cora. She'd caught on, and instead of bloodying his nose, she'd dabbed the corners of his mouth with a napkin, wiping a bit of chocolate protein bar off his lips.

Cora backpedaled—literally took three shimmery steps back—and once she retreated to the safety of her plaid-clad pack of loyal puppies, they closed ranks around her, tails metaphorically wagging, while she trash-talked me loud enough for half the dining hall to hear.

I mean, *please.* I hadn't binge-watched eight

seasons of *Psych* just to let a girl with glitter mascara and a superiority complex get the last word. Shawn Spencer taught me well: when they come at you with shade, you come back with a pineapple and some weirdly specific confidence.

"She probably thinks contour is a type of compass," I called sweetly across the table.

Ezra choked on his water. Annabelle froze mid-bite. Cory didn't even pretend not to smirk.

Cora turned with a blink, then tilted her head like I was a weird smoothie flavor she didn't order.

"Aw," she said, voice thick with sugar and superiority. "Ellie, it's adorable that you're trying to keep up. But this isn't campfire insult hour. It's called relevance. You should try it."

Her followers giggled on cue.

"Noted," I said with a nod. "I'll pencil it in between fighting crime and hunting turkeys."

She blinked.

Ezra whispered, "You've been watching too much *Psych*."

"Impossible," I whispered back. "I'm operating at peak Spencer."

Cora crossed her arms. "This isn't a CW drama, Ellie."

"No, you're right. If it were, I'd already have a tragic backstory and my own spin-off."

Annabelle choked on her juice. Even Cory looked impressed.

Cora took one last slow look at me, sizing me up like I was an unexpected stain on her otherwise flawless cafeteria seating plan.

"See you at The Test," she said finally.

I smiled like a girl who'd memorized *every single* episode of *Psych*, seasons one through eight, including the Halloween musical.

"Can't wait."

"Oh, I can," she said, pivoting with a sneer. "Just don't trip over your tree roots on the way in, forest girl."

"Don't worry," I said, grabbing my tray. "I've survived worse things than you."

"Like what?" she shot back.

"Turkeys," I said. "With claws. And zero interest in fashion hierarchy."

Ezra leaned in as she walked away. "You think she's going to win?"

I shrugged. "No idea."

Then I grinned.

"But I'm the one who knows I'm being tested. And unlike Cora? I brought snacks."

As Annabelle and I walked back to our dorm room to prep for the test, I re-read the invite:

Official Alliance Test Invitation

TO: E. Quinn

FROM: Alliance Performance Division

SUBJECT: Evaluation Directive – Tier One Candidate Assessment

You have been selected to participate in the Tier One Evaluation Protocol, effective immediately.

Participation in this closed-session assessment is mandatory for all selected candidates. The Evaluation will measure performance across four domains:

Cognitive Adaptability – strategic thinking under pressure

Physical Response – agility, precision, and endurance

Situational Obfuscation – improvisation and deception

Allegiance Verification – moral discernment and psychological compliance

LOCATION: Sector 9 Training Wing – Black Corridor

DATE: Today

TIME: 1600 hours (4:00 p.m.)

DURATION: Undisclosed

DRESS CODE: Standard Alliance Uniform – no additional gear permitted

NOTES:

Arrive alone.

Do not discuss this invitation with other trainees.

Surveillance will be active.

Failure to appear will result in permanent disqualification from advanced placement.

"Only the loyal rise."

—Alliance Evaluation Council

I swallowed hard. I'd already broken one of the rules: Do not discuss this invitation with other trainees. I felt like breaking another: Failure to appear will result in permanent disqualification.

All that sparring with Cora? Suddenly felt like yelling into a fan. Loud, pointless, and mostly for show. The Test wasn't about comebacks or cafeteria power plays. It was about something else—something bigger—and I still had no idea what. Maybe the smarter move was to run. Take whoever I could and bolt.

Problem: no one wanted out. They still thought The Alliance was here to save them, not use them. We didn't know what the EREBUS was. We didn't know what the mission was. And, not for nothing, I'd started wondering if Mom hiding me had actually fixed anything… or just let it rot longer. Like when you ignore a weird smell in the fridge and hope it goes away, but it doesn't. It multiplies.

I used to think she was hiding *me*. Now I wasn't

so sure she wasn't hiding *from* something—maybe from what she used to be. Maybe from Reggie.

Reggie had trained my mom back in the day—when she had been Caroline, the unstoppable operative. Back before the world had flipped, before The Alliance had taken root in the shadows and started poisoning everything we stood for. Back when Reggie had still believed in the system.

He had been more than just a trainer. He had believed in potential. He had believed in *her*. And when she fell—when she was accused of a murder she didn't commit and vanished into a prison cell like a ghost story—he had taken it personally. Like he'd lost the war by losing her.

And now? He was losing again.

The Alliance stole his last thirty recruits. Every teen he'd trained—gone. Just like that. And now he was unraveling. Guilty. Broken. Like a man who taught the right things to the wrong people.

And me?

I'm the final piece.

Maybe someone brought me here to finish the job. Not to shape me into a weapon—but to use me as the fuse. To destroy all three of us in one clean explosion:

My mother.

Brightwood Academy.

And Reggie.

And maybe it was working.

Unless I passed this test.

Unless I flipped the script before they lit the match.

———

At three forty-five, I dressed in my standard Alliance Uniform, an olive green job mimicking the armed forces garb. A yellow star on each arm and a blazingly obvious The Alliance emblem on the chest pocket. Annabelle lamented that she couldn't dress me up more or add some glitter to the drab pants and black combat boots. She'd settled for arranging my hair into a bun after I placed the issued cap on my head.

"I wish I could come and watch."

"Do you think Ezra will watch?" I asked, instead of replying to her wish.

"You really do have a crush on him don't you?"

"Yeah," I said, and let the blush rise up my neck to my cheeks. Admitting to a teen crush was better than saying "this whole capture by The Alliance thing is my fault, actually my mom's fault. They're going to kill me, kill my mom in prison, and then kill Reggie and close Brightwood for good. The Alliance wins."

Just before I stepped out the door, I thought better of keeping this all to myself. I needed my team and they needed to know my entire theory before I took The Test, which at this point, I'd convinced myself was code for my execution. Ezra hadn't had any issue securing the invite, and I think The Alliance orchestrated it.

Ignoring the failure to show clause, I ran back in the dorm room to my desk and grabbed a sheet of paper with The Alliance emblazoned across the top. I scribbled down a note for Annabelle to share with the team and drop in the mail chute afterward.

I thought The Test was about proving something. About rising up the ranks, earning a place, maybe even getting answers. But what if The Test was the final filter? The last round before they decided who was useful... and who was disposable. And if I'm right—if I'm even *close*—then my team is next.

Mom used to say survival isn't about strength—it's about spotting the trap *before* you step in it. If it looks too clean, too easy, too perfect? It's already sprung.

That's what this place felt like.

I couldn't prove anything yet. I couldn't prove all of it yet. But I could feel it—deep, like when the forest goes quiet and you *know* something's wrong even if you can't see it yet. I had instincts. I had patterns. I had Reggie's haunted face. I had thirty recruits who thought the Alliance chose them because they were special.

And now I had a test invitation that felt like a countdown.

So I did the only thing I could. I wrote it down.

Not some polished report. Not a formal complaint. Just the truth, the way I saw it, the way Mom taught me to spot it.

To the FBI – URGENT

From: E. Quinn

This isn't training. It's a takedown.

The Alliance placed me at Brightwood to finish what they started—

To destroy:

My mother (Caroline Quinn – wrongfully imprisoned?)

Reggie Cray (isolated, unstable)

Brightwood Academy (compromised from within)

The Test I've been selected for? It's not an evaluation. It's an execution.

Once I'm gone, my team—Ezra, Annabelle, Cory—will be next. They're being profiled for elimination.

Warn Reggie.

Get to my mother.

Shut down The Alliance.

I'll buy you time.

—Ellie

I folded the note and handed it to Annabelle.

"Get this to the mail chute right away." I leaned forward and gave her a quick hug. "Wish me luck."

I ran out the door and down the hallway, hoping she did exactly what I said and took the note to the mail slot. But I knew her well enough to expect her to be unfolding that note and reading it before I got to the doorway for Sector 9 Training Wing – Black Corridor. The doorway for Sector 9 clunked closed behind me. I stopped to catch my breath. However Annabelle was reacting to the note was out of my control. My secret hope was that she was showing it to Cory and Ezra and they were getting the heck out of this place.

Two black uniformed armed guards met me at the door to the Training Wing. I handed one of them my invitation and he looked it over. He raised his bushy eyebrows and handed me a card in return before opening the door.

I didn't look at the card right away.

I wanted to get a sense of the test center first—to read the room before it read me. I'd pictured separate stations: tactical puzzles, surveillance drills, maybe a moral dilemma disguised as a memory game. Classic spy school stuff. I figured the card in my hand would tell me where to start.

But there were no stations.

Just an octagonal room with matte black walls that seemed to absorb sound. Observatory windows lined the upper perimeter—darkened glass with dim lights behind them, like shadows were watching me from inside the walls.

One wall held a long, narrow table. Hand-to-hand combat weapons were laid out in neat, surgical rows: Knives. Batons. Throwing stars. And something that looked suspiciously like a garrote wire.

I took a step forward—and a door on the opposite side opened.

Cora walked in.

Hair flawless. Posture perfect. Face unreadable.

She didn't speak. She didn't need to.

My pulse kicked.

Only then did I unfold the card.

It read:

Tier-One Loyalty Assessment

Objective: Neutralize the opposing candidate.

Acceptable outcomes: Incapacitation or death.

Outside intervention will result in disqualification.

Noncompliance will be recorded as failure.

This is not a simulation.

This is The Alliance.

Kill your opponent.

I read it twice.

Then I looked up.

Cora reached the table and went straight for the knife. Not a training blade. Not foam, not plastic. Real. Slim. Double-edged.

Cora's blade slashed toward my ribs.

I barely blocked it with a baton. Metal met metal, and the jolt sang through my arm like a warning bell.

She meant it.

This wasn't a performance. This wasn't training.

Cora was going to kill me.

And I couldn't bring myself to strike first.

This isn't who I am.

Blood dripped from my arm. My muscles trembled, breath heaving in short, sharp bursts. We circled each other like animals in a cage—only mine was inside me, clawing at the walls of my chest.

I was going to die here.

And not just me.

They'd win.

The Alliance would take me out and bury Brightwood with me. My mother would rot in prison for a crime she didn't commit. Reggie would break, truly this time, and never recover. The last of the resistance would be smothered under silence.

All because I hesitated.

All because I wasn't enough.

"Ellie."

Her voice cut through the chaos—steady, firm, exactly as I remembered it from every back-woods sparring session and whispered midnight strategy talk.

"You know who you are. You know what they're trying to take. Don't give it to them."

My mother.

Not a ghost. Not a hallucination.

Just the part of her she trained into me.

"Get. Up."

My grip tightened.

Cora lunged—and this time, I didn't freeze.

I spun, dropped low, and swept her legs. She hit the mat with a cry, but rolled back fast, coming up with a snarl. Her blade flicked toward my side.

Too slow.

I slammed the baton into her forearm. Her hand opened, the knife skittering across the floor.

I aimed a second strike and stopped just short.

Cora stared up at me, panting, face pale.

"I yield," she whispered. "I yield. Please—just stop."

I stepped back, breathing hard. We'd both live. We—

The side door burst open.

Theo stormed in.

Eyes furious. Voice like a blade.

"She failed," he barked. "So did you. Finish them."

Two guards entered behind him, guns drawn.

"No!" Cora shouted. "She let me yield!"

Theo didn't even look at her. "Kill them both."

He turned to bark another order.

And I moved.

I lunged, baton raised, and drove it hard into his ribs.

He gasped and stumbled, clutching his side.

The guards rushed in.

And I froze.

Buzz.

Lassiter.

Gus.

The Chief.

Joan's men.

My monsters. My allies.

Brightwood's guards.

Not Alliance.

Brightwood.

They didn't hesitate.

The Chief snapped, "Secure the room!"

Buzz knocked Theo to the floor and cuffed him in one smooth motion.

Gus scooped up the card that had ordered me to kill.

"'This is not a simulation,'" he read aloud, his jaw clenched. "Yeah. We figured."

Lassiter helped Cora to her feet. She didn't look at me—but she didn't look away either.

I dropped the baton and let my knees hit the floor.

Not from injury.

From relief.

From the terrifying, shattering truth that I had survived.

And we weren't alone after all.

THE MED WING smelled like antiseptic and something vaguely lemon-scented. Ezra sat on the stool beside my cot while a nurse bandaged the gash on my arm.

He didn't speak right away. Just stared at the floor until the nurse left.

"You okay?" he asked finally, voice rough.

I shrugged. Winced. "Physically, or emotionally? Because I think the answer to both is no, but I'm sitting upright, so let's call it a win."

Ezra managed a tight smile. "You should've seen Theo's face when the guards didn't shoot."

"I kind of did. Right before I cracked his ribs."

He snorted.

"You saved Cora's life."

"She yielded," I said quietly, flexing my fingers, still half-expecting them not to work. "She was supposed to win. She was trained for it. Conditioned to believe she was chosen."

I took a deep breath.

"She didn't expect to lose. And when she did... I think she realized what she was really fighting for. That maybe The Alliance didn't choose her to rise—they chose her to be used."

I shook my head. "Even then, I couldn't do it. I couldn't finish her off."

Ezra leaned in slightly. "You didn't just pass The Test, Ellie. You rewrote the rules. People saw what happened in that room. We've got it on camera. We can use that."

"To convince the others?"

He nodded. "To show them what The Alliance really is."

I swallowed. "Then we get them out."

"We will," Ezra said. "But you should rest. You're the fuse, remember?"

I raised an eyebrow. "Not sure I love that nickname."

He grinned. "Yeah, well, you lit the match. Let's just make sure the fire hits the right target next."

———

The infirmary lights buzzed overhead, flickering just enough to be annoying. My arm pulsed under layers of gauze, every heartbeat a reminder that I'd made it out—barely.

Ezra crouched beside the bed, fingers flying over his tablet like he was conducting a symphony in Morse code. Cables snaked from his device to the wall panel behind him, tapping directly into The Alliance's main grid.

"You sure this'll work?" I asked, voice still rough. Might've been the blood loss. Or the fact that I'd just survived an almost-execution.

Ezra didn't look up. "If it doesn't, we're out of time and options. But yeah. I'm sure."

He tapped a final key. The tablet screen blinked once—then settled on a countdown. Five seconds. Four.

He turned to me. "You ready to watch the truth go viral?"

I nodded. "Let's crack it wide open."

Every screen in The Alliance Training Center went dark—just for a second, long enough to make the silence feel loaded.

Static crackled across the monitors.

Then came the card Cora and I had received, bold and center screen.

"This is not a simulation. Kill your opponent. Failure will not be tolerated."

Footage of the fight played next: My baton. Her blade. My blood on the floor.

Then came Theo—storming in like a villain ripped from a bad spy movie.

"She failed. So did you. Finish them."

"Kill them both."

The last image: me, battered, bloodied, staring straight into the surveillance cam.

"If we're weapons, they'll use us—until we're empty. Then they'll bury the evidence."

Ezra clicked on the keyboard, and the cameras he'd placed throughout the training center played like a live-action reel across the laptop screen at the foot of my infirmary bed.

In the cafeteria, someone dropped a tray. Forks paused midair. Cereal went soggy in bowls. No one cared.

In the gym, girls in matching leggings and matte lipstick stepped off treadmills, eyes fixed on the glowing monitors.

In the training halls and dorms, it was the same. Some froze. Some whispered. A few started moving.

Not toward their assignments.

Toward each other.

Toward the truth.

While I was still stuck in the infirmary—arm wrapped like a burrito, head pounding like I'd head-butted a freight train—my team kept me in the loop.

Cory filled me in first. "Damica's been slipping coded messages into archive folders," he whispered, glancing at the closed infirmary door. "She only hands them off to people we trust. One by one, kids are vanishing from sight—heading underground."

Annabelle dropped by next, smuggling in a protein bar and sass. "Cory and I swept the dorms," she said, unwrapping the snack like a spy movie heroine on a lunch break. "He knocks, I pass out wristbands—color-coded signals for who's in. Also, tell your glitter pen it's doing the Lord's work."

Ezra crouched beside the bed later, dark circles under his eyes, tablet still warm from use. "Adelina led the evac team through the old service tunnels," he told me, fingers drumming nervously on the metal railing. "She looked like she walked straight out of a heist film—matte-black gear, zero hesitation. Jim and Kat gave the go-ahead before the sweep started."

"Two minutes to lockdown. Perimeter secured," Ezra mimicked, his voice dropping to match Kat's calm precision.

Then he added, quieter, "Father Raphael's at the tunnel exit. Handing out prayers like shields. Shaking hands like he means it."

My voice—my face—was still on every screen.

The video had struck the match.

For the first time since walking into this place, I didn't feel like a pawn.

I was the fuse—and I was already burning.

———

I wheeled my duffel bag into the same marble hall I'd stumbled through what felt like a lifetime ago. Except this time, I wasn't looking for an escape route. I wasn't wondering who the other "broken" kids were or whether I belonged.

I knew who I was now.

And I knew exactly what Brightwood really was: not a group home, but a resistance movement disguised as luxury and structure. A training ground for kids like me—kids with secrets, scars, and survival stitched into our bones.

"Need help with that?" Ezra appeared beside me. His titanium legs clicked softly—shoes or not, the sound carried in the quiet tiled hallway. His curls were a little longer now, and whatever uncertainty weighed his shoulders before had fallen away. Confidence? Clarity? I wasn't sure. But he was steadier now.

I handed him the bag. "Only if you promise not to give me a speech about low-tech luggage being inefficient."

He smirked. "No promises."

We passed the full-length mirror, and I caught my reflection again. Same red hair. Same freckles. But the girl staring back looked older, like she'd walked through fire and came out with teeth bared and armor in her eyes.

We weren't just pretending anymore.

"You okay?" Ezra asked, quieter now, his voice a

bit more like the boy who'd set up my DVD player on day one.

"I think so." I glanced out the window toward the lawn.

The tennis courts were full. The gazebo was surrounded by new recruits laughing over some kind of team-building exercise that involved fruit and sabotage.

"We got them out, Ezra. All of them."

He nodded. "Footage ran on every screen for two straight hours. Theo's 'kill them both' moment kind of tanked his approval rating."

I snorted. "Shame."

We turned down the corridor toward the main hall. It smelled like cinnamon and fresh paint—like someone was trying to erase the shadows of everything that had happened. But some stains don't scrub out. And maybe they shouldn't.

Cory and Annabelle stood by the stairwell, looking like they hadn't just survived an overthrow of a covert criminal network. Annabelle still had her signature eye roll loaded and ready. Cory's smirk was back to 75% capacity.

"You ready for this?" Cory asked as we walked up.

"Define 'this,'" I said.

"The part where we all pretend we're just a bunch of teens hanging out at a boarding school with killer surveillance tech and a secret underground resistance," he replied.

"I've been pretending since I could walk," I said. "Now I'm just pretending louder."

Annabelle arched a brow. "Still think I should've taken your spot at The Test?"

I met her gaze. "You were amazing. But I had to go through that. I needed to see what I was really capable of. And what they were willing to do to us."

Silence for a moment.

Then she said, "Well, I'm glad you didn't die. That would've really messed up the vibe."

Cory looked around and lowered his voice. "Any word on Theo?"

"Last I heard, he's somewhere deep under lock and key, screaming into the void about loyalty and legacy," I said. "The usual."

Ezra grinned. "And Reggie?"

"He's… healing. Slowly. But he's here. He's helping. That's something."

I turned toward the bank of windows, the lawn beyond dotted with new faces. Some scared. Some angry. All of them watching the rest of us to see if we knew what we were doing.

Spoiler: we didn't.

But we knew who we *weren't*.

We weren't The Alliance. We weren't pawns. And we weren't done.

Father Raphael strolled across the garden, deep in

conversation with Jim. Kat and Adelina stood near the edge of the tennis court, coaching two new trainees. Brightwood was full now. Full of noise and questions and the quiet kind of hope that comes after the world cracks open and doesn't fully close again.

"We did it," I whispered.

"For now," Ezra said. "But the EREBUS—"

I shook my head. "One mission at a time."

And yet… I couldn't shake the image of that device. Hidden in the archives. Waiting.

The kind of secret that doesn't stay buried.

I reached into my jacket and pulled out the note I hadn't shown anyone yet. I'd found it tucked inside one of my mom's old training books in the library. One word. Scrawled in my mother's careful, almost military handwriting.

EREBUS

I looked at my team—Ezra, Annabelle, Cory— and felt it in my bones.

The war wasn't over.

It was just changing shape.

———

You survived Brightwood.

But that was just orientation. Grab the next book!

EREBUS Protocol

NOTES

CHAPTER 14

1. Agatha Christie, *The Murder of Roger Ackroyd*

Copyright © 2025 by Kathleen Guire

All rights reserved.

Kathleen Guire, Author supports the copyrights of human authors. Thank you for reading an authorized edition of this book and for complying with the copyright laws by not reproducing, scanning, or distributing any part of it in any form without written permission from the author. You are supporting writers. For more copyright information, please write to contact@kathleenguireauthor.com.

This is a work of fiction. Names, characters, businesses, places, events, locales, and incidents are either the products of the author's imagination or used in a fictitious manner. Any resemblance to actual persons, living or dead, or actual events is purely coincidental.

No part of this book may be reproduced in any form or by any electronic or mechanical means, including information storage and retrieval systems, without written permission from the author, except for the use of brief quotations in a book review.

Cover by Beckanddot

Edited by Megan Sebaaly, Charming Chapters

ABOUT THE AUTHOR

Kathleen Guire is the mother of seven, four through adoption, NiNi of fifteen, former National Parent of the Year, author, teacher, and speaker. She loves connecting with readers through her website (Kath leenguireauthor.com).

For more information,
about Kathleen, check out her website and follow her
on social media!
www.kathleenguireauthor.com
kathleenguire@gmail.com
https://linktr.ee/kguire

www.ingramcontent.com/pod-product-compliance
Lightning Source LLC
Chambersburg PA
CBHW020138310726

48970CB00006B/1924